HAUNTED LIFE OF DELORES MACKENZIE

Yvonne Banham

First published in 2024
by Firefly Press
25 Gabalfa Road, Llandaff North, Cardiff, CF14 2JJ
www.fireflypress.co.uk

A CIP catalogue record of this book is available from the British Library.

ISBN 978-1-915444-66-0

This book has been published with the support of the Books Council Wales.

Printed by CPI Group (UK) Ltd, Croydon, Surrey, CRO 4YY

For my big sister, Carol

1

Delores pressed her nose up against the window of the taxi as it rumbled over the cobbles of Edinburgh Old Town, desperate to catch the first glimpse of the Tolbooth Book Store. She'd had enough of hiding, and more than enough of the notorious Witches of Harris, Prudence's mother in particular. The witches were supposed to be their guardians during the Inquisition, give them a safe hiding place while the paranormal rift caused by Delores earlier that year was investigated. But Prudence and Delores quickly found out that the witches possessed only a meagre smattering of hedgewitchery and were keener on squabbling and thieving than looking after two fourteen-year-olds.

As Delores caught sight of the Tolbooth's clock-tower, she flapped her hand at Prudence.

'I can see it! I can see it!' she squealed, but Delores'

hand dropped as fast as her stomach when the taxi pulled to the side of the road. The shop was in darkness and its heavy oak door was shut tight.

Delores searched her coat pocket for her last five-pound note. They should have walked the short distance from the station, but Prudence was in pain and even more broke than Delores. Prudence's mother had taken the last of her money, leaving her burning with shame as she kicked them out of her cottage. She'd said it was to cover costs, but both girls knew she'd already been paid a small fortune to take care of them. And now, furious about the short trip, the driver added a random premium; Delores' last fiver wasn't enough.

Prudence cleared her throat and smoothed her hands over her coat. 'My friend's just going inside to get some money from our guardian,' she said, nudging Delores into action.

The driver narrowed his eyes at Delores through the rear-view mirror and reached for the central locking button. She gave him a weak smile and hopped out while she still had the chance, dragging both suitcases behind her.

By the time she'd rattled the Book Store door handle for the third time, Prudence was standing next to her, and the taxi was on its way back down the cobbles of Canongate.

‘I could have got him the money,’ said Delores.

Prudence shrugged. ‘You were taking forever. I planted a simple illusion in his head, and he seemed happy enough. It’ll wear off by the end of his shift and maybe he won’t be so gruesome to his next customers. Why are we still standing in the street?’

Delores took a deep breath and bit back a sarcastic reply. They were tantalisingly close to Cook’s delicious food and crisp, clean sheets, to the roaring fire, the books; even their lessons with Uncle Oddvar were an exciting prospect. Until she’d been left in Oddvar’s care, Delores had thought of the Uncles as creepy weirdos, scrabbling around libraries and museums, greedily gleaning information over their freakishly long lifetimes; all so they could *educate* young Paranormals in the laws and legends of their society. Oddvar was strict, obsessed with his rare books, but equally kind and loyal. He’d made it clear to Delores that simply speaking to the dead was acceptable but allowing them to use her extraordinary levels of necromancy to re-join the realms of the living was not.

And in the underbelly of the Old Town that spring, one of the reluctant dead, a Bòcan, had almost made it back. It had caused a ‘paranormal rift’; that and rescuing their classmate Maud from the shadowlands of death. Oddvar had called it *necromancy beyond acceptable limits*, and he warned there would be trouble from the paranormal authorities: an Inquisition. But he still did everything he could to protect her. Sending her off to Harris with Prudence to get them out of the way had seemed like a safe bet, an adventure, but Delores missed the Tolbooth and everyone in it way more than expected. She jiggled the handle again and gave the door an impatient kick. Maybe they weren't expected back today. Worse still, maybe they weren't expected back at all.

'What if…?'

Prudence glared at her, but Delores knew it was now or never. 'What if your mother was lying when she said it was safe to come back? What if the Inquisition isn't over? We could be—'

'Putting everyone in danger?' snapped Prudence. 'Thanks for pointing out my mother's probably a liar as well as a thief.' She nudged Delores out of the way and knocked hard on the door with the side of her fist.

Delores peered in through the shop window, shielding her eyes to cut out the reflections from the streetlights and passing cars. 'Maybe there's a simple explanation, like … Oddvar's gone out?'

'*Like Oddvar's gone out*?' mimicked Prudence, rolling her eyes. 'Not while there are Normals wandering around. Honestly, Mackenzie, I've met goldfish with better recall than you. And even if he had, where's Gabriel? I still can't get him to open his mind to me. So annoying.' Prudence took an elaborate blue-green key from the zip-front of her suitcase and tapped Delores on the nose with it.

Furious, Delores made a grab for the key. 'You didn't think to mention you had that?'

Prudence snatched the key backwards. 'It's ancient, and not an exact fit. To anything. It needs expert handling.' She bobbed down with her ear next to the keyhole and inserted the key, blinking slowly with each click-shunk-click of the lock's barrels. 'We're in.'

Prudence pocketed the key, grabbed her case from Delores and stepped inside.

Delores was about to follow when a bone-achingly cold hand touched the base of her skull, where her close-shaved hair left her skin exposed. She breathed deeply, gathering her strength as a sharp nail traced a thin line down from her occipital bone to the first knobbly protrusion at the top of her spine, stopping at the first curve of the markings hidden below her scarf.

Delores grasped the back of her neck. She spun round, ready to push back whatever random ghoul had touched her, back to where it belonged. A partially formed figure flickered at the edge of her vision before melting into the darkening street. Lingering in the autumnal air, like a charge of electricity, was the feeling that the reluctant dead; the Bòcain, knew that Delores Mackenzie was back in the Old Town.

This time, Delores was ready for them.

She took a small piece of blue chalk from the deep, newly hand-sewn pocket inside her coat and drew a troll cross on the wall next to the door. She carefully traced a loop that crossed its lines at the bottom, curling back on itself to make two smaller loops: a charm to keep the dead outside. She placed her hand over the mark, hoping the small amount of witchery she'd learned from Prudence's mother over the summer would be enough to activate its ghoul-repelling properties. She said the words softly, 'This is our shield. This is our domain. We alone determine who shall pass.'

Feeling quite pleased with herself, Delores tripped on the step and staggered forward into the darkness of the Tolbooth Book Store.

2

Delores reached along the wall to find the light switch. She flicked it a couple of times, but nothing happened. A festival poster, half-pulled from the wall, wafted in the cold air from the street as Delores' eyes adjusted to the eerie abandonment inside. Stacks of boxes stamped with the name of their book supplier sat unopened and the old-fashioned cash register was slumped on its side with its drawer gaping open. Sheets had been thrown across the book tables, and paperbacks lay scattered and rumpled underneath.

Delores looked around for Bartleby, wondering why the little demon gargoyle wasn't in his usual spot. He should have been guarding the door, demanding blue sherbet straws from them in exchange for safe passage.

'Barts!' she shouted, panic itching at her throat.

Prudence held her hand out to shush Delores. There was a snuffling, sobbing sound, the gentle jangling of chains and a few choice words in French.

They followed the noises to where Bartleby had always slept in his basket, snuggled under his best baby-blue blanket. Delores' toe reached the edge of a dense black space, and she knew instinctively not to take another step. The sobbing stopped and there was a deep, guttural sniff.

Prudence waved her hand in front of the black void. 'Interesting.'

Delores side-eyed Prudence. Only Prudence would find any of this *interesting.* The dark space made Delores squirm. She put her hand to her mouth to quell the feeling of motion sickness as the darkness swelled and receded. She would have stepped away, but she could hear something moving inside the dark and the gentle grinding of stone teeth. 'Bartleby?'

Delores waited, listening to soft, rasping breaths from inside the dark, until a familiar gravelly voice said, 'Oui, ma petite, I am here. But you? You should not be.' Bartleby reached out of the darkness. His grey-white wrist was manacled, and a metal chain trailed along his arm.

Delores knelt and pulled him towards her.

Bartleby stumbled into Delores' arms. She cradled

his head against her chest and tenderly rubbed his back. She could feel the notches of his spine and the sharp edges of his shoulder blades beneath her fingertips. 'What happened to you?' she whispered.

The little gargoyle jangled his chains. 'I, Bartleby L'Aubespine, demon of the lower orders, je suis *prisonnier*!' His eyes were wide and brimming with tears. His toothy jaws trembled.

'He said he's a *prisoner*,' said Prudence.

'Thanks, genius. Worked that one out all by myself,' sighed Delores. She put her hand under Bartleby's chin. He ran his fingers along a crack in one of his stubby horns. 'I hide in this darkness I made. But *she* still hunts my secrets, she hunts *all* our secrets. I keep them safe.' Bartleby tapped each of his ribs with his index finger, counting as he went, as if the secrets of the Tolbooth were inside, safe next to his heart. 'The questions … they hurt my brain. *She* hurts my brain.'

'Who? Who hurts you?'

Bartleby cupped Delores' face in his hands. His palms felt cold and rough against her skin. 'You must go,' he said. 'You must both go far away before … before…'

Bartleby froze mid-sentence as the door between the shop and the private rooms at the back creaked open.

‘Uncle Oddvar?’ whispered Delores.

‘It’s not Oddvar,’ said Prudence. Her voice was low and uncertain. ‘I’d know if it was him.’

The door opened fully, and an unfamiliar voice said, ‘Welcome back to the Tolbooth Book Store.’

With a finger-click, the lights snapped on. Delores scrunched her eyes shut. The Tolbooth was a place of soft lights, lamps and candles, not harsh, glaring brightness. Prudence leaned against Delores’ shoulder so gently it was barely a touch, then spoke to her inside her thoughts with an urgency bordering on panic.

Something’s wrong. Really wrong.

Delores used everything Uncle Oddvar had taught her. She slammed down her mental shutters, protected her thoughts from unwelcome attention. She opened her eyes slowly, afraid to see what monstrous thing could have freaked out the steadfastly unflappable Prudence S-Dottir.

A woman peered at them from the doorway. Her face was disturbingly neutral with small features clustered around its centre. Her eyes shone like tiny buttons under a milky forehead, void of eyebrows, and her glossy black hair was drawn back so tightly it looked as if it might pull itself out by the roots. She was dressed head to toe in shades of black and charcoal grey.

She wore a shirt fastened high under her chin, a velvet waistcoat and thick, soft felt trousers – all covered by a tightly fitted tailcoat of crisp, two-toned taffeta. The soft cuffs that hung below her sleeves drifted like torn spider webs, and her alabaster hands reminded Delores of the marble angels that stood guard over graves.

Bartleby slunk back into his little patch of darkness, muttering prayers and curses in equal measures of French and Latin.

The woman stared at them in silence and the longer the silence went on, the more pressure Delores felt to speak. Words clambered from her thoughts and bundled up behind her tongue, desperate to break free. She choked back the impulse to explain why she and Prudence had come back, to confess to her battles with the reluctant dead, about the transgressive nature of her necromancy, but her ability to control her mind and her mouth was slipping away fast. The strange woman's gaze never left her. Delores felt compelled to say something, anything, to break the tension. 'Did you do this to Bartleby?' she blurted. Speaking words out loud brought a wave of relief but her momentary willingness to tell this stranger her darkest secrets left Delores sick with anxiety.

The woman smirked and then winked at Delores. 'Never mind, we have plenty of time.'

The smirk and the wink sparked fury in Delores' chest. 'Take those shackles OFF him,' she shouted, gesturing towards Bartleby's dark sanctuary, 'Or when Uncle Oddvar gets back he'll … he'll…'

The woman looked over her shoulder, then back at Delores. 'What makes you think the Uncle has gone anywhere?'

'Because he'd never put up with this. Bartleby is family!'

The woman laughed. 'Family? The gargoyle is a deception, a demon as despicable as The Morning Star himself. He has no legal place here.'

'You're wrong,' spat Delores. She could feel Prudence agitating beside her. She was sure Prudence would step in any minute. Prudence would do something. Plant a super-scary illusion. And now would be really excellent timing.

The woman smiled as she leaned against the door frame with her hands in her trouser pockets. She took out a pocket watch and checked it with an air of boredom. 'I don't think you understand who you're dealing with,' she said. 'I am Magoria Jepp, Senior Inquisitor, tasked by the Psychic Adjustment Council with the investigation of Paranormal Malfeasance, of a spike in paranormal activity just streets from here. I'm assuming you're the necromancer, Delores

Mackenzie? And you,' she said, nodding towards Prudence, 'must be the illusionist.'

Prudence held Magoria's gaze, unblinking. Delores spotted the tip of Prudence's tongue pressed between her teeth, a clear signal she was planting an illusion inside this infuriating woman's head, and as soon as she ran away screaming, they'd free Bartleby and…

Prudence's voice cut into Delores' thoughts, bringing them to a screeching halt, *I can't do it…*

'Nice try, Illusionist,' said Magoria. 'Clearly you haven't dealt with an inquisitor before.' She gestured towards the back room with her head. 'Tarry no more, we have matters to discuss.'

'Tarry?' muttered Delores. 'What kind of loser says *tarry?*'

'She's no loser,' answered Prudence. 'She's one of the Old Ones. Like Oddvar.'

As Magoria turned and walked back through the door, it was clear they were expected to follow.

Prudence leaned in close to Delores. 'She bothers me. I can't get past her defences or see what she's thinking. I put an illusion in her head but … nothing, zilch, nada…'

'What did you try?'

'A Hercules beetle. Every perfect detail: beautiful

horns, exposed wings. I even added its tiny white eggs on her…'

Delores raised her hands. 'I know what your best beetle work looks like, thanks. Maybe she's not scared of them.'

'I wish. She knew it was an illusion. I know she could *see* it, but it just crumbled into nothing. I couldn't make her *believe*. There's something super-dark about her, something I can't quite get a grip of.' Prudence shuddered. 'Keep her out of your head, Mackenzie. If she sees what you did to get Maud back from the hands of that dead thing, we're done for.'

Delores' mouth opened but she couldn't say the word.

'Do I have to do all the work?' asked Prudence. 'She'll call a Gathering.'

The mention of it chilled Delores to the bone. It was how her parents had disappeared. No trace, no answers, other than what Oddvar had told her. *North,* he'd said, impossible to find, non-existent in the eyes of the High Council that governed all Paranormals from their seat in Norway. The only things she knew for certain was that they were taken in the night while she slept, accused of crimes against their society, of stepping outside the bounds of acceptable paranormal activity, just like Delores had.

Prudence's fingers drifted to the nape of her neck. She adjusted her soft paisley headscarf to cover the barb of a freshly formed feather. 'We all have something to hide,' she said. 'The trick's going to be getting rid of Magoria Jepp before she finds it.'

3

The room behind the shop was as dimly lit as Delores remembered but, instead of the carefully curated shelves and glass cases, precious books had been taken from their homes and stacked next to a ledger on the central table. Other books had been pulled out halfway on the shelves and abandoned. It gave the room an irregular look and Delores wanted to pass through it quickly. She decided that Oddvar must have left; he'd never allow this to happen.

Prudence stopped at the glass case containing Oddvar's most precious *Compendium of Demonology and Visitants*. Her shoulders tensed as she ran her finger through the dust on the surface of the case. She held it up to show Delores the dirt she'd collected. Oddvar handled the *Compendium* every day, it was his obsession, but the glass case hadn't been opened in some time. An unsettling thought rumbled against the mental barrier Delores was fighting so hard to keep up; maybe Oddvar was a prisoner too. Magoria caught the slip in Delores' concentration and turned back to face her with a sly smile. Prudence stepped between them, giving Delores vital seconds to regather her focus.

'Ah well,' said Magoria. 'I don't need to get to work on you straight away.'

As Magoria continued towards the stairs, Prudence tapped Delores on her temple.

Delores pushed her hand away. 'I have TOLD you not to do that! Like *ever*.'

'Keep your guard up then! At least until we know what we're dealing with.'

Delores nodded. Prudence was right, and as much as it irritated her, at least that one thing was normal.

Upstairs the enormous open fire cast a warm flickering glow across the dining room as wood cracked and spat sparks amongst the flames. Delores' heart leapt as she caught sight of Uncle Oddvar, sitting in his chair next to the fireplace, and again on seeing her friend Gabriel for the first time in what felt like forever. He was sitting on the floor leaning against Oddvar's legs, glasses pushed to the top of his ruffled white hair as always. She dropped her bag and pushed past Magoria to get to them, trying not to find it too weird when Gabriel didn't get up or even look excited to see her.

'Gabe! We're back!' Delores threw her arms around his shoulders, but Gabriel kept his eyes on Oddvar, barely acknowledging she was there.

'You shouldn't be here,' he whispered. When he noticed Magoria staring at them, Gabriel shrugged Delores off. He nodded at Prudence, and Delores thought she saw a fleeting exchange between them, too quick for the inquisitor to catch.

Despite the heat from the fire, Oddvar's legs were wrapped tightly in a thick woollen blanket. His neat black boots poked out from the bottom; his ankles pressed together. His eyes were closed, and his hands had been placed on the open pages of a book, as though he might wake up and start reading at any moment. His monocle was wrapped in his slender fingers and his black nail varnish, usually the height of glossy perfection, was dull and outgrown. Delores watched him for a moment to check he was breathing, holding her own breath tight in her chest. Seconds seemed to stretch into minutes but finally his chest rose, then slowly fell back into a deathly stillness.

Delores put her hand on Oddvar's, but there was no response. His pale skin felt dry and papery against hers. Its usual greenish hue was tinted grey. She squeezed his hand gently and whispered, 'Uncle, it's me, Delores.'

Delores looked more closely at Oddvar's face. His eyes were firmly shut, and there were no flickering thoughts or dreams beneath his eyelids. Reflected in the firelight, Delores noticed an almost transparent network of silken threads stretching across Oddvar's face, denser in some parts as they twisted themselves into delicate webs. The threads wove their way past his cheeks, thinning towards his neck. The finest of them reached in silver-spun tendrils to his shirt collar and from his wrists to his sleeves. Delores reached out to touch them, but Gabriel shook his head and lowered her hand with his own.

'How long has he been like this?' Delores asked, looking from Gabriel to Magoria in disbelief.

Magoria checked her pocket watch again, as if that might hold the answer. 'Long enough,' she said. 'He still has questions to answer, and failing that, I'll have him removed as he is.'

'Removed?' Delores could feel tears brimming but she refused to let them come. 'He's an UNCLE.'

Magoria winced. 'I would thank you to lower your voice. This is all Oddvar's own work.'

Magoria leaned over the top of Delores and

whispered in Oddvar's ear. 'You old fool. They came back anyway.'

Magoria lingered close to Oddvar's face, her breath ruffling the looser tendrils that were working their way around his earlobes. Delores felt a physical unease deep in her brain matter, like phantom fingers rifling through thoughts and prodding at memories. She hoped the feeling was Gabriel or Prudence trying to make contact, but this felt new and more intrusive. Her head was flooded with relief when Magoria moved away.

Gabriel touched the back of Delores' hand, drawing her attention back to the moment. She caught a dark thought rippling quickly across his face before he replaced it with a weak smile. His reading of her was complete. 'You think you left the dark thing outside the door?' he whispered, glancing up at Magoria.

Gabriel turned back to stare at the fire, and Delores knew he'd said all he could for now. She patted Oddvar's hand and whispered, 'Later, Uncle.'

'Come on,' said Prudence. 'Let's go unpack.'

'How are you not seeing this?' Delores gestured towards Oddvar with her head.

'I see it,' hissed Prudence. 'Let's put. Our stuff. In our rooms. This can wait.'

Magoria held her hand in the air. 'That would be *room*. Singular. The one next to the clocktower.'

Prudence stood upright, shoulders back. 'I have my *own* room. The one next to Gabriel.'

'She's right,' said Delores. 'I share the room next to the tower with … Maud.'

As soon as the name left Delores' mouth, an awareness of Maud's absence, so sharp you could almost touch it, was left hanging in the air.

'Where is she?' whispered Delores. Her eyes searched the darker recesses of the dining room as if their younger house mate might jump out and surprise them any second.

'Maud's gone,' said Gabriel. He gave Prudence and Delores a look that said *don't ask*.

'So,' said Magoria, 'go to your *room* and get some rest. My questions will continue in the morning.' She half-smiled and gestured them away with both hands. Delores felt a push between her shoulder blades, a kind of psychic shove to get her moving.

Delores staggered forward but Prudence dug her heels in. Her face was red with anger. 'That's assault,' she snarled.

Magoria laughed darkly. 'Oh child, you are in for a few surprises if you think *that's* assault.'

Prudence's whole body tensed as she took a

small step towards Magoria. Delores wracked her brain for some kind of distraction, something to diffuse the situation before Prudence lashed out. Prompted by her stomach rumbling, she asked, 'What about dinner?'

Magoria breathed out slowly and spoke without taking her eyes from Prudence. 'I have instructed Cook there are to be no meals outwith my specific timetable. Dinner has finished.'

'But it's not even seven. Dinner is at seven,' whined Delores. She'd expected a welcome home bowl of Cook's finest stew at the very least. Just the thought of it made her jaws ache. She looked towards the kitchen in the vague hope that Cook would appear and save the day. There was a suggestion of movement in the shadows, then nothing. Defeated, she picked up her bag and headed for the corridor that led to the clock tower's spiral stairwell, relaxing a little as Prudence joined her.

As they passed Gabriel's room, they could see it hadn't changed over the summer: orderly, simple. A small pile of books sat on his bedside table, his tarot cards next to them, pristinely stacked and tied with ribbon. The troll cross they'd scratched into the floor outside his door to protect him in the spring was still there. Magoria had either missed it, or she didn't care.

Delores crouched down and ran her fingers over the marks. There was still a faint buzz from the charm Prudence had used to activate it.

'How much do you think Gabriel remembers?' whispered Delores. 'You know, about the attack? That Bòcan only attacked him because of me.'

Prudence quickly put her finger to her lips, shushing Delores. 'Enough of the pity party,' she whispered, pulling Delores back up by her sleeve. 'If it helps, I doubt he remembers anything, or Magoria would have found it and we'd already be sunk.'

A few steps further along, the door to Prudence's old room was open. It was clear that Magoria had taken it. She'd kept the expensive rugs, the beautiful star charts and the telescope given to Prudence by her father Solas, but everything else was gone. The bed was covered in animal pelts, snowy white, and chestnut brown, deep russet and silver-grey, some with their heads still attached. Delores counted at least two arctic foxes before looking away in disgust. 'Do you think those are real?'

Prudence looked back towards the dining hall. Magoria was too busy settling herself into the chair opposite Oddvar to pay them any more attention; the cosy cushion-filled armchair where Prudence's father, Uncle Solas, had always sat. 'Definitely looks like someone who'd collect skins off dead things,' she answered.

As they walked along to the snug where Solas had had his nest, his books and his artifacts, Delores lightly placed her hand on Prudence's shoulder. All evidence of Solas' life as a shapeshifter, his day-to-day existence as a bird, had been swept clean.

'They're not expecting him back, are they?' said Prudence. Her voice was wet with tears.

'Maybe Oddvar and the others did it,' said Delores. 'Keep anything incriminating away from Magoria. You weren't expecting him to be here, were you?'

'Not really. Part of me hoped after he left us with my mother, the least he would do was…' She swallowed hard. 'I can't keep my barriers up much longer and if I'm struggling, you'll be a liability.'

'I'm not completely useless,' said Delores.

'If you say so. I can still feel her probing, like she's putting little feelers into my brain.' Prudence shuddered. 'We'll see if there's a line where she loses us. A dead zone.'

'Very funny.'

'You're welcome.'

Delores held open the door to the next stairwell and they dragged their bags in silence to the room at the top.

4

Delores' room looked much the same as the day they left for Harris, except that all traces of Maud were gone, swept away as thoroughly as Solas had been. Even the creepy dolls Maud was so fond of were nowhere to be seen.

Delores wrapped her mother's scarf around a small bird skull that she took from her pocket, then placed it carefully on her bedside table. She always carried the skull with her on her travels. It had been a gift from her father and reminded her of home, her real home, no matter how far she went. She pulled her shirt collar up and fastened the top button, checking the edges of her skin markings were well hidden from Prudence. The marks had appeared after her first real battle with a Bòcan. What had looked like the simple frost that forms on glass had morphed into slender fronds that reached onto the side of her neck and down her back. She was afraid of them, of what they could mean, but she loved the comfort of having something deeply private: a precious commodity when it felt like the living and the dead watched your every move. She knew she would need to share them if she was ever to understand what they meant, but with Oddvar out of action, her options felt limited. For now, they would stay hers, and hers alone.

The silver ball that Oddvar had given her was still in her pocket where she always kept it and the bell in its centre tinkled as she threw her coat on her bed. Even though he was closer to her than he'd been all summer, it was now that she missed him most desperately. All her other unpacking was just stuff that could wait.

Prudence examined her new bed. She lifted the corner of the downy quilt then dropped it with a sigh before checking out the jumble of belongings that had been dumped from her old room into boxes left roughly stacked by the clocktower door.

Delores peered over Prudence's shoulder at the contents of the uppermost box. There was a bound copy of *Alice in Wonderland* on the top. Its spine was broken, and the front cover was forced back on itself. The pages inside were crumpled and foxed with mildew. Prudence ran her hand over a smudged inscription on the first page. 'My grandmother gave me this.'

Delores tried not to react. She was always shocked that Prudence had family. First Solas, then her mother. Now this.

'What?' said Prudence, snapping the book shut.

'You've never mentioned a grandmother before. Is she from the witchy side? Or was she a shapeshifter?'

'Does it matter?' muttered Prudence. She picked up the remains of a smashed bottle of perfume from the box, then dropped it back in. She wiped her hand on her pinafore. 'It's ruined. All of it.' She dabbed under her eyes with her shirt cuff.

'The boxes underneath might be OK,' said Delores.

'Not if *she's* touched them.'

Delores reached for Prudence's shoulder but pulled back at the last second. Prudence had never been a hugger, but since the first few feathers had broken through the skin around her scapulae, the pain caused by touch was physical as well as emotional. Prudence's shapeshifting was a work in progress, new and a little frightening without her father to guide her through it. Her mother had been worse than useless when she'd found out, not even trying to hide how freaked she was. She'd offered everything from the flight patterns of early morning birds to the slightly more disturbing toad song as evidence that it was safe for Delores and Prudence to return to the Tolbooth, and Prudence had been eager to believe her mother's witchy predictions. Getting away from the woman who'd discarded her once already was way more appealing than the cosy white cottage or the never-ending, star-filled skies of Harris could ever be.

Delores thought it kinder to change the subject, even if it was back to the inquisitor. 'Is Magoria still prowling around your thoughts?' she asked. 'I'm too tired to focus on anything much but I can't feel any creepers or feelers or fingers or whatever.'

Prudence closed her eyes and gave a weary sigh. 'Me neither.'

Delores flopped backwards onto her bed, breathing in the flowery fabric softener mixed with the musty age of her quilt. It was a heady mixture, calling her to the realm of blissful sleep. 'We can try and find out what's going on tomorrow,' she said. 'If we can't get anything much out of Gabriel, there's always Doctor Reid. Someone must have been helping him care for Oddvar, and Oddvar did say before we left that Doctor Reid would be helping with our lessons at some point.'

Prudence nodded. 'A plan that's nearly useful. Well done!'

'I have my moments.'

Prudence arched her eyebrow at Delores, and she caught a fleeting glimpse of the old Prudence, the brilliant, prickly, infuriating sort-of-friend-but mostly-not that she missed so much.

From inside a restless sleep, Delores heard the tower's clock mark three with whirrs and clicks. She was drifting back down into velvet oblivion when she felt a hand on her shoulder. It startled her, but then she relaxed again at the warm tenderness of its touch. When her eyes drifted shut, she felt a gentle shaking. Someone whispered *Wake up.* As she forced herself awake, she could make out Gabriel's blond hair turned silver by the moonlight from the window.

'We need to talk while we have the chance,' he said.

Delores propped herself up on her pillow. Prudence was already awake, a silk shawl draped over her shoulders. She could see the outline of Prudence's shoulder blades – bigger than they should be, angular and jutting, but their sharpness was increasingly softened by the feathers that insinuated themselves through her skin day by day. Delores' secrets weren't the only dangerous ones. Both governments, Paranormal and Normal, had outlawed shapeshifting in any form. They called it *subversive* as it lent itself so beautifully to crime, deception, and uprisings. Going all the way back to the infamous Jack the Ripper, shapeshifters were left to perish in the prisons of the North; their children sent to die alongside them until it could be proven that the ability had not been passed on. It was growing more obvious each day that Prudence had inherited her father's shapeshifting Gift, and a Gathering would sweep Prudence up alongside Delores if Magoria caught wind of those feathers. Delores instinctively adjusted the collar of her pyjamas, checking her markings were covered. If only hiding things from Magoria was as simple as that.

Gabriel nudged Delores' arm. 'Earth to Delores.' He smiled and passed her a mug of hot chocolate. It was just how she liked it: tiny marshmallows floating on a raft of soft fluffy cream with a chocolate flake broken and scattered amongst them. She wrapped her hands around the mug and inhaled the love put there by Cook. The first sip was bliss.

Gabriel pulled a package, carefully wrapped in greaseproof paper, from his dressing gown pocket and gave it to Delores. She tugged gently on the delicately tied teal ribbon. As the ribbon loosened, the paper sprung open revealing three buttery cookies infused with cinnamon. 'Do I love Cook right now, or what?' she said, mainly to the cookies.

Prudence moved gingerly to Delores' bed, bringing her own gifts from Cook with her: soft ginger biscuits cut into stars and her own luxurious hot chocolate, the top layer sticky with melted Turkish delight. She gave her own thanks to Cook, then turned to Gabriel. 'Easier if you say it out loud. For the sake of the less gifted amongst us.' She smirked, then gestured to Delores that she had something on her upper lip.

Gabriel snorted into his drink. 'Glad to see nothing's changed between you two.'

Delores wiped away a gooey chocolate moustache with the back of her hand. 'Plenty's changed around here while we were away. Care to fill us in?'

Gabriel pulled gently at his hair, twisting the ends into spikes as he gathered his thoughts. 'I remember waking up and you two were gone. It's a blank before that. I couldn't figure out why Doctor Reid was feeding me *disgusting* medicine while Oddvar told me exactly nothing. Great summer!'

Delores opened her mouth to speak but Gabriel put his hand up to stop her. 'Don't. I can't tell the inquisition what I don't know. Magoria showed up, ranting about a rift in the Paranormal Sphere, hell-bent on speaking to you, Delores, massively agitated about undeclared necromancy. It didn't take much to connect the dots to Maud; us thinking she was dead.

There were a couple of others with her at first, but she soon sent them back north. Sorry, it's all a bit of a jumble and doesn't make sense because Maud was at the Tolbooth, same as always. Except…'

Delores' hand hovered near her mouth with her half-eaten cookie. 'Except what?'

'She *wasn't* the same as always. Oddvar was twitchy when she was around. He tried keeping us apart, but I grabbed her hand at breakfast one morning, did a reading.'

'And?' Delores took a nibble of her cookie, sweeping a stray crumb in with the side of her finger.

'And nothing,' said Gabriel. 'I couldn't see any future, just grey mist and weird shadows. I thought it was me at first, like *I* couldn't read her for some reason. So, I told Uncle Oddvar and he totally weirded out. Never seen him like that. He arranged for her to go to Uncle Barnabas in St Andrews before Magoria could do anything to stop him. Haven't heard a whisper about her since.'

Delores and Prudence shot each other a look. When Delores opened her mouth to speak, Prudence stopped her.

Delores almost dropped her cookie in frustration. 'Maud wasn't ever—'

'Stop!' growled Prudence. 'And don't do any

readings on either of us, Gabriel, just in case you see something you shouldn't.'

'Bit late for that,' said Delores through the remains of her cookie. 'He already did one, didn't you, Gabe?'

'Not really,' said Gabriel. 'Just checking you out. I *thought* I remembered liking you, but I needed to be sure. Like I said, everything's confusing.'

Prudence rolled her eyes. 'Can we move this lovefest along?'

Gabriel shivered and pulled his dressing gown more tightly around his chest. 'When Magoria realised Maud was gone, she went at Oddvar, like full-on crazy stuff. He put up a fight but he's … you know … *old* old. They had a massive argument. I've never heard Oddvar shout before but the whole building was vibrating, books falling from shelves, jars of stuff in the kitchen exploding. Next thing he just…' Gabriel shrugged, struggling to find words to describe it. 'He shut himself down, like he was hibernating. Magoria is *proper* raging. She might not show it, but she is.'

'That woman oozes rage,' said Delores. 'Maybe she got too close to something Oddvar couldn't let her see.' She drained the last of her hot chocolate then wiped her finger around the sticky rim of the cup to gather up the last of the melted flake. 'Have you used your skills on Uncle Oddvar? You touch his hands all the time. You must have seen something.'

'I've tried,' said Gabriel. 'Every morning at first, but I just saw the same thing over and over.' He closed his eyes, visualising the image before speaking it. 'A giant moth, resting in the dark. Sometimes I get glimpses of fancy patterned walls and this big red heart. Not a real one, like a jewel or a sculpture or something. But mainly the moth.' He looked at them again, nodding at their puzzled expressions. 'I know, right? I would have asked Doctor Reid about it, but Magoria's always there and I'm not leaving Uncle alone with her, obviously.'

'Obviously,' said Delores and Prudence in unison. They looked at each other half irritated, half amused.

Delores took another biscuit. 'What about Bartleby?'

'Magoria found his secrets. He kept ours hidden at his own expense. That's when she chained him up. We begged her to let him go, but every time we asked she shortened his chains. She even took his chess pieces.'

Delores offered her last cookie to Prudence, feeling relieved when she refused it. Delores finished it in two bites then pressed her sticky finger into the last few crumbs on the paper. 'Can't Cook do anything?'

'Too busy guarding Cook-shaped secrets,' said Gabriel. 'How was your summer with the witches?'

Prudence cringed at the word. 'You'd know if you'd bothered to find out,' she said.

Gabriel flinched. 'I knew you were with your mother, and Oddvar banned us from contacting you. He was keeping you safe the best way he knew how. It was hard enough hiding your location from Magoria without adding messages to the mix.'

'Well wow, thanks then,' muttered Prudence. She folded the paper from her cookies with furious precision, sharpening the edges with her fingernails until it resembled a tiny bird.

'Don't be like that. I thought you were with your...' Gabriel glanced at Delores. 'I mean Uncle Solas.'

'Delores knows Solas is my dad,' said Prudence, 'but he left for the North when the witches got suspicious about his shapeshifting. They are SO ignorant. He thought we'd be fine to stay on without him. But you can see how that worked out.'

In the silence that followed, the whirring, clunking of the clock sounded four broken chimes. Gabriel looked towards the door and tilted his head. 'Magoria's stirring. Hardly sleeps.'

'Hearing's as sharp as ever,' whispered Delores. 'What about your eyesight?'

Gabriel shrugged and Delores knew not to ask any more. He was at the door when he turned back to them. 'Stay out of each other's thoughts; Oddvar said she senses when our minds are open. She'll start small. You'll feel compelled to tell her something and believe me I choose that word carefully. Have some small safe secrets ready. But they must be true. She pounces on lies, plays with them until you tell her something she wants to hear.'

'What do you mean *plays with them?*' asked Prudence.

'It's like she's fumbling through your brain,' said Gabriel, 'and if that doesn't work, the pain starts. Saying nothing won't work either.'

'Bring it on, Magoria Jepp,' smirked Prudence.

'Don't even joke, Prudence,' said Gabriel. 'She's vicious. Why do you think Oddvar's in the state he's in? This isn't like when the Uncles take a sneaky peek at what we're thinking; it's an actual Inquisition, like the one's we're taught about in class, ones that end in jail … or worse. You'll feel her inside your brain, like she's sorting through files.'

'I already did,' said Delores, 'when I was with Oddvar. It was grim.'

Prudence reached up to her shoulder, feeling for the soft feathers through her shawl.

'Don't worry,' said Gabriel, 'that secret's buried deep, but she's getting closer.'

In the dim light, Delores saw what little colour Prudence had drain from her face. She nudged into her gently with her shoulder. 'Relax. My brain was too full of Oddvar and Bartleby for her to find anything about you. And as you're always telling me, not much room in there at the best of times.'

Prudence smiled into her mug.

'It is good to have you back,' said Gabriel. 'Magoria was never going to give up, not before she got what she wanted.'

'And what is that exactly?' asked Delores. 'She doesn't know about Prudence and I'm total small fry. Why put all this time and energy into a bit of dodgy necromancy?'

'That,' said Gabriel, 'is an excellent question.' He raised his mug at them then disappeared into the stairwell.

Prudence went back to bed. 'We should get some sleep,' she said. 'We're going to need it.' She picked up a book from her bedside table, a strange old book she'd read repeatedly during their summer on Harris. It belonged to her mother and was filled with illustrations of warty trolls and small, fairy-like figures: changelings that were swapped with real children, leaving their parents distraught. Delores wondered whether it was because Prudence hated being her mother's daughter, or because she was too afraid to be her father's. Now they were back at the Tolbooth, they had every book they could wish for, but Prudence still clung on to that weird old thing.

Delores slid back under the covers, certain she wouldn't sleep, eyes wide open until they weren't. She was sinking slowly, carried along on a gentle lullaby sung by a strange distant voice that broke in parts, words falling away. *Prudence? Singing?* she wondered. There was a first time for everything.

5

When Delores came back from the bathroom, Prudence was already dressed and had a fresh silk scarf wrapped around her hair like an annoyingly cool bandana.

'Very "earth-child",' said Delores, making quote marks in the air with her fingers.

Prudence frowned in reply then held two cream satin ribbons out in front of her.

'Can you tie these around my wrists? Feathers on the breakfast table might be hard to explain.'

Delores sat on the edge of Prudence's bed. 'Have you got some spare secrets lined up just in case?'

'Of course. You?'

'Yep. Kind of.'

Delores twisted the ribbons into soft bows. Prudence examined her handywork, and when she was vaguely satisfied, she rummaged under her bed and pulled out three dolls. 'Are these Maud's?' she asked. 'I thought I heard something scratching around under there, but when I looked all I found were these hideous things.'

Delores groaned. 'No, not Maud's. Not exactly. Can I have them?'

Prudence handed them over with a shudder. 'Whose are they and when can you give them back?'

Delores put her hands around the dolls. The prickling hairs on her arms and the back of her neck were a warning that their ghostly owner had stayed after Maud's departure. She held them to her face for a closer look. The dolls' glass eyes stared into the space behind her until Delores whispered, 'You don't fool me.' The dolls blinked in unison. There was a subtle click of eyelids and their tiny button noses crinkled in disgust as they glowered at Delores. She blew the dolls a sarcastic kiss and carried them to the door that led from their room to the clock tower. She placed each one face down on the step. 'They used to belong to someone called Agnes,' she said. 'Maud told me Agnes didn't like it in the graveyard.' She inclined her head towards the clock tower door.

'You're not serious,' whispered Prudence. She glanced at the dolls and away again. 'I thought that troll cross chalk thing kept them out?'

'Not if they were already in. Or if they died here or...'

Prudence put her hands up to stop her. 'Like it's not bad enough sharing a room with *one* spooky freak.'

'Rude,' said Delores. 'You didn't seem to mind it last night when you were singing that weird song.'

'Have you ever heard me sing?'

'No but...'

'Do I look in the mood to sing? Is there anything about me that makes you *think* I might want to sing?'

Delores couldn't stop her eyes flickering towards Prudence's hairline.

'Don't even go there,' snapped Prudence. She opened the bedroom door and ushered Delores through, whispering *weirdo* as she passed.

Gabriel and Magoria were already seated at the dining table, Magoria at its head. Oddvar was still perched death-like next to the roaring fire. Delores and Prudence skirted around Magoria, bending to whisper *Good Morning, Uncle* in Oddvar's ear, before making a show of taking their places at the table opposite Gabriel, their backs to the fire.

Cook had already been hard at work and a gentle hug of delicious aromas embraced them. Their favourite thick, soft toast covered in salty butter was waiting on their side plates and Gabriel stood to offer them porridge from the giant silver serving dish. They both nodded and he ladled a generous portion into their bowls. Delores added some cream; Prudence tasted hers first then added a pinch more salt. Neither of them acknowledged Magoria but watched discreetly as she cut the top from six tiny pale-blue eggs. She used a slender fork not much bigger than a darning needle to peel away the whites and then scoop out the hard yoke with surgical precision. She placed the yoke onto dull black crackers, never once looking up. 'It's rude to stare,' she said. 'I trust the morning finds you well?'

'Yeah, great,' muttered Delores.

Magoria wiped her mouth delicately on a pristine napkin, paying particular attention to the corners. She refolded the napkin and bent to take a book from a sealskin satchel that rested against the legs of her chair. She dragged out a heavy ledger and dropped it onto the table with a bang, delighting as Gabriel jumped at the noise. Delores and Prudence clung tightly to their porridge spoons, their appetites lost. They'd all seen the ledger before. It had a mid-brown fabric cover with a darker but modern binding. Its bold bronze lettering glistened in the morning firelight: *The Tolbooth Book Store: Habitant.* Their names and details had been added shortly after their arrival and the book wasn't taken out again unless an adjustment was required, like a new skill emerging, or a student sent away. The book was a harmless document, a register Oddvar never used. He knew who lived at the Tolbooth and who did not, and he knew most everything about them.

Delores looked at Prudence. Prudence shrugged in reply, taking a slow, sliding mouthful of her porridge.

Magoria took a delicate pair of wire-framed glasses from her upper pocket, the lenses not much bigger than her bead-like eyes. With her glasses balanced on her tiny nose, she opened the book halfway in and ran her finger down the page. The gold lacquer on her nails caught the light as she searched the lines of text, her hands deathly pale against the soft creamy page.

'Registered in March,' she said. '*Delores Mackenzie*, Necromancer. Singular Gift. Disappointing.' She looked over her frames at Delores. 'Unless of course, you've been doing more than simply communicating with the dead.'

Delores quickly returned to her fascinating bowl of porridge, thinking up a harmless scrap of truth to distract Magoria if she looked any deeper. Magoria lifted her glasses and examined the text more closely, adding a salting of sarcastic disbelief. 'Youngest daughter of Magda and Dillan Mackenzie? Oh dear. We have a dark seed amongst us.' She licked the tip of her finger and flicked back to the previous page.

'Wait,' said Delores. 'What do you know about my parents?' Delores hated the desperation in her voice, and that Magoria would have heard it.

Magoria didn't bother to look up. 'I know enough to be suspicious of you, Necromancer. Single skilled? We shall see.'

Delores shifted uneasily in her chair, desperate to ask questions, reluctant to let Magoria have more power over her than she already had.

'Next,' said Magoria. 'Oh yawn … Gabriel Galbraith. I've already had quite enough of your tiresome company, Master Galbraith, though your charming little display with Ms Mackenzie yesterday was vaguely interesting. Don't think it went unnoticed.' Magoria gave a self-satisfied grin and went back to the book. 'According to this, you possess *strong divinatory skills through touch* and have *that most common form of Divinator's Curse: impending loss of vision*.' Magoria looked over the top of her glasses at Gabriel. 'Also some minor telepathic ability, but I know Oddvar warned you away from using that particular Gift around me.' She traced her finger along the page. 'I see the Galbraiths have a long history of Divination Associated Morbidity. How tragic.' Magoria lingered on the last word.

Gabriel's face was ashen. 'I'll go unlock the door for Doctor Reid,' he whispered. He took a piece of toast as he pushed back from the table, nibbling the corner as he caught Magoria's eye.

'The toast had better not be for the gargoyle,' said Magoria, half distracted by the entries in the register.

'Of course not,' mumbled Gabriel, but Delores knew from Gabriel's blushes that Bartleby would be getting some breakfast. She hid a smile behind her porridge spoon.

As Gabriel disappeared down the stairs, Magoria continued with, 'Maud. Well, we all know *she's* not here, though quite why that's the case, we have yet to ascertain.'

Prudence gasped as Magoria took a red pen and put a violent line through Maud's name. She tilted the book towards them. 'Which brings us to Prudence S-Dottir, Illusionist, noted Telepath with undesirable displays of telekinesis under duress.' Magoria traced the words again with her finger, reading slowly. 'Prudence. S. Dottir.'

Delores wasn't sure where Magoria was going with this, but it wasn't anywhere good. Prudence put her hand up to her temple and pressed her fingers hard into the bone.

'You OK?' asked Delores.

Prudence dropped her hand to her side. 'I'm fine. Everything's under lock and key.' She looked sideways at Delores, blinking slowly and Delores knew to keep her guard up.

'If I may continue?' said Magoria. 'Your mother is Senga Pennyroyal of the Harris Witches. Correct?'

Prudence nodded. Small beads of sweat were gathering on her upper lip. 'It's quite warm in here,' she said.

Magoria gave both girls a tight-lipped smile. 'How mortifying for you, to have a witch for a mother, even worse for that witch to be Senga Pennyroyal.'

Prudence shifted in her seat and dabbed her face softly with her ribboned cuff.

Magoria did not miss it. 'So that's where you were,' she said, 'with the Harris Witches. How naughty of them not to report it.'

Delores placed her hand on Prudence's arm and squeezed gently.

'I'm fine,' hissed Prudence.

Magoria peered at the words on the page as if they had become much smaller. 'Yet here you are, not Prudence Pennyroyal as one would expect, but

Prudence S-Dottir, a shortening of the Icelandic patronymic naming system. So that would make you Prudence, daughter of…? Who *is* your father, Prudence?' There was an added slyness to Magoria's tone – a snake waiting to strike.

Delores watched wide-eyed as Prudence's mouth formed an S against her will. The next sound was hovering behind it when they both jumped at the sound of boots running up the stairs. The moment shattered as Doctor Reid rounded the stairwell, her long tweed coat swishing behind her. Her presence filled the room from floor to vaulted ceiling; even the cherubs and angels carved into the dark-wood bookshelves lifted their faces in delight at her arrival.

'That's quite enough, Magoria,' said Doctor Reid. 'You're not here to investigate the parentage of Oddvar's students. As dear Uncle would say, that is quite *outwith* your remit, as am I, so don't try any funny stuff.'

Doctor Reid marched towards the dining table, bringing a wave of damp autumnal air with her, pausing to place a gentle kiss on Oddvar's cheek. She unravelled her long woollen scarf and draped it along with her tweed coat across the back of the chair opposite Magoria. She ruffled her white cropped hair, pulled the chair out and flopped down onto it. She slung her arm over its back, exposing her delicate porcelain wrist bones. When Delores caught Prudence staring, Prudence blushed and looked intently at the ribbons on the ends of her sleeves.

'Gracious,' said Doctor Reid, 'looks like Cook was expecting me. Clever Cook.' She smiled at Delores and Prudence, raised her eyebrows twice then nodded towards the side plate that had appeared while their attention was on Magoria. She gestured politely at the silver coffee pot as Gabriel arrived back at the table. He poured a steaming cup full to the brim while Doctor Reid bit enthusiastically into her toast. Delores had only seen Doctor Ernaline Reid once before but had remembered every detail. Ernaline was wearing the same crisp white shirt, high necked and ruffled, her legs covered by a long, full skirt and thick stockings. Her skin looked powdery, and her cropped white hair was an unusual texture – like the slender scales that make moths fuzzy and soft.

'Lepidoptera,' whispered Delores under her breath. As if she heard her, Doctor Reid flashed Delores another quick smile before taking a second bite of her toast. Delores would file that word amongst her favourites, just like she had already with the name *Ernaline*.

Doctor Reid returned her defiant gaze to Magoria.

Magoria closed the book and ran her hand over its cover. 'Good morning, Ernaline,' she said through gritted teeth.

Doctor Reid waved her toast at Magoria and nodded a greeting in return.

The relief that came with Doctor Reid's arrival didn't last. Delores could see the physical tension building in Prudence's body. She was sitting stiffly in her chair, shoulders pressed against its high back. Delores winced at the thought of those tender shoulder blades against the hard wood.

'I tricked the cab driver yesterday,' blurted Prudence. 'I planted an illusion in his head, paid him with chocolate coins.' Her body sagged as the words tumbled out.

Gabriel dropped his spoon and Delores looked at Prudence, mouth agape.

Prudence shrugged. 'You know I had no cash. Don't worry, it was decent chocolate.'

Magoria sat back, one arm draped over the high back of her chair, sarcastically mirroring Ernaline. 'A minor truth,' she said, smiling, but her face betrayed her. She'd been close to something dangerous. 'Do you feel better, Prudence?' she asked. 'Most Paranormals do when they surrender a truth.' Magoria leaned towards Prudence. 'Do you feel unburdened, Ms *S-Dottir*?'

'No, not particularly.' Prudence picked up her spoon and smoothed the scarf that covered her hair with her other hand. A feather escaped from the nape of her neck and drifted down to the table. Delores smacked her hand on top of it. Everyone turned sharply to look at her.

'I hate flies,' said Delores. Magoria could have that truth free of charge.

Doctor Reid watched Delores' hand until she slid it from the table, taking the feather with it. 'I should take the girls under my wing,' she said. 'Oddvar shows no signs of recovery and they're entitled to an adult to act in their interest. Oddvar named me Guardian in his absence. Check with the legal department.'

Magoria smiled. 'How very strange he should think to do that. However, I'm fully capable of—'

'Of what? Questioning them to the point of exhaustion? Even the Psychic Adjustment Council has rules governing an inquisition, Magoria. I must insist on taking care of their general welfare starting with a trip to the tailors.' She waved her coffee cup in Prudence's direction, then brought it back for a delicate sip.

Magoria's eyes flickered as she made a brief appraisal of Prudence: her ill-fitting pinafore, too tight across the chest; her plain shirt stretched over her shoulders, exposing taut stitches. Her gaze lingered momentarily on the ribbons at Prudence's wrists before adjusting the cobweb cuffs of her own shirt. 'Do go on.'

'I think a trip to Cormican, Bunsby and Cavalletto is called for.'

'Ah yes, Cormican's,' said Magoria, 'outfitters *extraordinaire* in every sense. I was planning a visit myself.'

Delores slowly took a spoon of porridge, eyes never leaving Doctor Reid. She'd heard of Cormican's. She'd even passed by it on the way to the Grassmarket Vintage Emporium, but she'd never been inside.

Doctor Reid's eyes ran down the length of Magoria. 'You don't look in need of a visit to the outfitters.'

'It won't be a social call,' said Magoria. 'I hear the nephew is displaying some troubling behaviour.'

Doctor Reid inhaled sharply, before recovering her composure. 'The boy is young. I'm sure the Cormicans know what they're doing.' She turned to Gabriel. 'Will you join us on our outing?'

Gabriel shook his head. 'I'll go with Uncle Oddvar when he's better.'

Doctor Reid placed her hand on his arm. 'I'm sure Oddvar would like that very much. Just me and the girls then.' She glared at Magoria, daring her to object.

Magoria slipped the book back into her bag.

‘The Mackenzie girl has only displayed a gift for necromancy: single-skilled thus far. As such, she is low status and not entitled to *specialised* garments.’

Delores scraped her bowl hard with her spoon.

‘She can come along for the jolly then!’ said Doctor Reid, taking another bite of her toast. ‘Go get ready, girls. I need to check on Oddvar, but let’s be away in twenty minutes, yes?’

Prudence pushed her chair back. ‘Gladly.’

As Delores got up to follow, Magoria grabbed her by the wrist.

Delores focused on blocking Magoria out of her mind, on keeping her away from her darkest secrets. Magoria laughed. ‘I’m not looking for anything, silly girl. You’ll know when I am.’ Her eyes flickered towards Prudence as she sunk her fingers deep into Delores’ wrist.

Delores tried to pull away. ‘You’re hurting me.’

Magoria let go, smiling as she reached back into her bag. ‘This came for you.’

Delores snatched the envelope. It was her sister Delilah’s handwriting, post-marked Tromsø, Norway, and dated over a month earlier. She gripped the edges of the envelope so tightly they buckled.

‘I could have sent it on, if only I’d known where you were,’ said Magoria.

Delores felt an already familiar nudge in her shoulder, ushering her away as Magoria went back to excising her miniscule egg yolks, placing them with tender precision onto her weirdly disgusting black crackers.

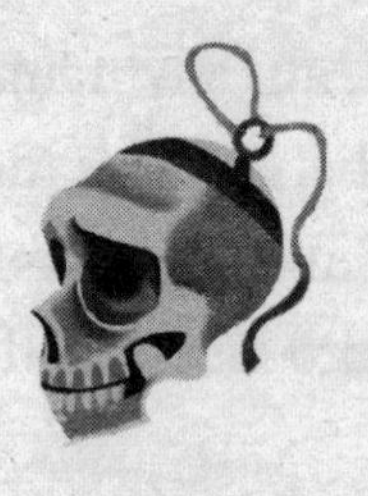

6

Delores sat on the edge of her bed looking at the envelope, tracing the curling capital letters and running her thumb over the stamp.

'Open it then,' said Prudence. 'You've been waiting to hear something all summer.'

Delores tapped the letter against her hand. 'What if it's bad news about my parents?'

'Then at least you'll know.' Prudence knelt behind Delores on the bed. 'Want me to read it?'

Delores thought for a moment. It might be easier hearing what Delilah had to say in Prudence's matter-of-fact tone. The words might sting less. She took a deep breath and handed the letter over.

Prudence cleared her throat. 'She says work's going well, her mentor at The High Council seems to like her, but she has little freedom and no connections yet at the department of … wow

… the Department of Illusory and Treacherous Mislocations?'

Delores nodded. 'They supposedly investigated my parents' disappearance, but they were very selective in what they told us. Delilah had already been planning her career with the High Council, so when Mum and Dad vanished *she* reckoned it made even more sense to go. Great for her, not so great for me.'

'We're not that bad, are we?' said Prudence, sounding almost sympathetic.

Delores smiled. 'Suppose not. What else does she say?'

'*So, no news yet. They wouldn't let me send cash. The Normals here don't allow it. But I've wired money to the Uncles, you just need to ask them for it.*'

Delores sighed. 'Great. Don't suppose you found any money tucked away in your box of stuff?'

Prudence shook her head and went back to the letter. 'She says something about developing new skills but doesn't say what, then just *stay well*, stuff like that.'

Feeling disappointed at the lack of Delilah's progress, Delores took the letter and slid it under her pillow. 'Doctor Reid must be waiting by now,' she said.

Delores stepped out of the Tolbooth into a drenching mist that quickly covered every inch of her in tiny glimmering pearls of water. There was an eerie glow as the autumn sun tried to burn its way through the silver-grey, but she hoped it would fail; the mist had such an Edinburgh Old Town vibe about it.

Doctor Reid and Prudence were busy fastening their numerous coat buttons when Delores' attention was drawn to Esme's Sweet Shop across the road. Tumbles of Halloween pumpkins and squashes adorned its step and the flickering candles inside their carved centres cast an amber glow in the strange light. As Delores moved closer, she saw Esme through the mist, staring at them. Esme had always been kind, always interested, but Delores and Prudence had barely paid her any attention other than to buy treats for Bartleby.

When she caught Delores staring back, Esme bobbed down and tended to the Halloween display, rearranging two of the minor pumpkins before dashing back inside and slamming the door. The familiar shop's bell cut sharply through the damp air before being swallowed whole.

Delores checked her pockets for that last fiver. She might regret it, but Bartleby deserved a treat.

When she stepped inside the sweet shop, Delores was enveloped in a blanket of welcoming warmth and delicious smells that perfectly matched the season; the coconut and caramels of the spring had given way to cinnamon, aniseed and burnt toffee. Delicious treats that whispered of autumn chills and the long months leading to Christmas.

Esme had dashed to her safe space behind the counter. Her immaculate red lipstick and rolls of platinum blonde hair made Delores conscious of her own appearance. The droplets from the mist dripped from her long fringe, rolled down her nose, and gathered into one big drop on the end of it. She wiped her sleeve across her face and cleared her throat.

Esme feigned surprise at Delores' presence, flashing a huge smile. 'Blue sherbet straws?'

'Please. Six.'

Esme put the straws into a paper bag, scrunching the neck of it and tying it with a twist of black and white thread.

Delores reached for the bag, but Esme held on to it. 'I miss you kids coming in,' she said. 'No one else buys these things.' She let go of the bag with a nervous laugh. 'I thought maybe the boy would come in at least. Gabriel, isn't it? Always so polite. But I rarely see anyone leave the shop these days.'

Delores dipped her head and offered Esme the five-pound note for the sherbet straws.

Esme refused the money. 'First treats of spooky season are on the house. Are you going to the festival?' She pointed over her shoulder at a poster advertising the Samhuinn Fire Festival taking place on Halloween night in the parklands next to Holyrood Palace. The fiery letters danced beneath a dramatic photograph of the ruins of St Anthony's Chapel looming high on the hillside above another year's celebrations.

'Halloween?' Delores hoped Esme wasn't thinking they might go together. Slightly tragic, even for a friend-free zone like Delores. 'That's … tomorrow.'

'It's only a five-minute walk at most,' said Esme. 'I'm sure your … *guardian?* would let you go. It's super-fun, dancers, fire-eaters, you'd love it.'

Delores tucked the money back in her pocket. 'I know. I've been before. With my mum.' Her voice cracked on the last part.

Esme blushed. 'I don't mean to step on any toes.' There was an awkward silence before Esme leaned across the counter, as if she were about to share some massive secret. 'Do you know about the spirits of The Five?'

Delores shook her head, not quite sure where Esme was going with this.

Esme grinned. 'According to Edinburgh legend, they were murdered and their ghosts dance at the chapel ruins, the one in the poster. Only at Halloween mind, when the veil between the living and the dead is at its thinnest.' Esme then ruined the whole thing by doing spooky hands with added sound effects.

Delores wondered if *The Five* was one of the stories that leaked between the Paranormal and Normal world. Edinburgh had a whole industry of ghost walks built on them, but she was curious to know exactly what Esme meant. 'You can see them?' she asked. 'I mean, you specifically?'

Esme turned her attention to the gleaming toffee apples in the display cabinet under the counter, dressing them with black jelly spiders and spun-sugar cobwebs. 'Not *actually*, but I do have a sixth sense about these things. And about people.' She looked intently at Delores, waiting.

Delores felt a nervousness creeping in. 'How do you mean?'

'You kids. And the old guy. The funny-looking one. You're different.' Esme's hand hovered above a gleaming candy-red, crispy-coated apple. The jelly spider trembled between her fingers. 'If you ever need a friend...'

Delores could hardly breathe. Esme had to be guessing, picking up on their *oddness* like the girls at her old school did. She looked closer at how Esme was dressed, searching for clues. Her clothes were nothing like Doctor Reid's, or Uncle Oddvar's. Certainly nothing like Magoria's.

Delores was about to ask her exactly what she meant when Esme slipped her hand inside her apron pocket and pulled out her smart phone to check the time. No Paranormals could use tech without destroying it. Esme was a Normal, a nice one, but a Normal all the same.

'Thanks for the offer,' said Delores, 'but we only just got home.' She was tucking the bag of straws safely in her pocket when the door flew open. Prudence grabbed her arm and dragged her back out onto the pavement without so much as a *Hello* to Esme.

'How long can it take to buy a few sherbet straws?' Prudence kept a firm pincer grip on Delores' arm as she marched her up the street, trying to catch up with the surprisingly hare-footed Doctor Reid.

7

By the time they reached the curved terrace of Victoria Street, the crowds of tourists were emerging from their hotel breakfasts and enough sun had burned through the mist to show the pastel rainbow of shops at their gorgeous best.

Smells of freshly baked bread tumbled from Tilly Whitlock's bakery as they passed, mixed with the sticky-sweetness of biscuits topped with thick fondant and finished with blood-red cherries. Delores was about to suggest a quick purchase, but a few steps ahead Doctor Reid had stopped at a discreet metal gate, set slightly back from the street. She glanced over her shoulder then opened the gate, urging the girls to follow her into a narrow cutting. Delores trailed her hand along the damp wall and her skin prickled. She checked behind her but there was nothing there.

At the end of the narrow passageway was the door to Cormican, Bunsby and Cavalletto. The names were artfully painted above the dark polished granite doorway in gold script.

Delores, Prudence and Doctor Reid stepped into the void beyond the door. For a few seconds there was only darkness and a strong urge to turn back, but when their boots reached the polished oak floorboards, the shop slowly revealed itself. Instead of a roaring fire like the one at the Tolbooth, there was a clutch of pyramid-shaped heaters with flickering blue flames that gave off a smell like the ice-cream van at Holyrood Park. The walls were lined with shelves of ankle boots of every colour, made from shiny patent or soft, supple-looking leather. They had covered buttons up the sides or were criss-crossed with straps and chunky buckles. There were glass cabinets filled with gloves and scarfs, cravats and stockings, next to bags, wallets and pocket watches. Tailored coats were displayed on headless mannequins, their gold, silver and verdigris buttoned cuffs pinned across their fronts. Some mannequins had long skirts like Doctor Reid's, others sported the narrow pinstripe trousers favoured by Uncle Oddvar. Delores' heart lurched as she thought of him.

She felt Doctor Reid's hand on her shoulder. 'Glorious, isn't it? Take a closer look. See what appeals to you.'

Delores shrugged. 'Is there much point?'

'Time will tell,' said Doctor Reid, 'but there's no harm looking. Let me know if you feel a connection to any of the items. It might be an indication of things to come.'

'I don't think they're destined for the bodies of Paranormals with singular Gifts,' said Delores.

Doctor Reid put her arm around her and squeezed. 'But what a Gift you have my dear. Maybe afternoon tea will cheer you up. I know the concierge at the Caledonian.'

Delores smiled at the thought. 'That'd be great,' she said, 'but Cook won't be pleased.'

'Cook won't begrudge us a few cakes,' said Doctor Reid, 'not in the circumstances.' She winked and then shone her full attention on Prudence. Delores tried not to die of envy, but she believed she just might.

A softly squat woman bustled out from behind the shop counter to greet them. She had a measuring tape slung around her neck and a gleaming pair of scissors that jangled from a chain. The chain was attached to a thick leather belt that cinched the waist of a dull-brown corduroy dress. Her owlish hair was heaped on the top of her head in a messy nest, and her feet were engulfed by enormous fluffy slippers. Delores liked her instantly.

Doctor Reid kissed the woman on the cheek, then introduced her to Prudence and Delores as Ainsley Cormican, *most fabulous designer and friend to every Paranormal in Edinburgh.* A ruddy-faced man with tufts of black and silver hair tutted from behind the counter as he unfolded a paper pattern for a waistcoat and held it in the air in front of him.

'And that's her husband, Balgair.' Doctor Reid cast a dismissive gesture towards the man with her hand.

'Oh, never mind Old Misery over there,' said Ainsley. 'Who do we have here?'

'This is Delores Mackenzie, and this is Prudence ... *Solas*dottir,' said Doctor Reid.

Delores noticed Ainsley's left eyebrow arch as she uttered a questioning 'oh?'

'Prudence,' said Doctor Reid, 'is having some difficulty navigating the arrival of her ... feathers.'

Delores watched Ainsley's face for a reaction. The lack of one made her wonder just how common shapeshifters were in Edinburgh.

Balgair sighed heavily from behind his paper pattern. 'Your trade in the extraordinary will be the end of us, Ainsley Cormican. Humans shapeshifting into birds indeed. Or is it the other way round? Criminal, some would say. That girl's father…'

Ainsley silenced her husband with a vicious look before turning to Prudence. She put her hand under Prudence's chin and her face softened into a concerned smile. 'We'll have you looking and feeling incredible in no time,' she said.

Once everyone seemed oblivious to her presence, Delores turned her attention to a rail of tailored trousers. She didn't normally buy new stuff, she loved her charity shop finds, but for these beauties she could make an exception. As she ran her hand over a pair made of soft, mossy tweed, there was a rattle of coat hangers from the shadows at the rear of the shop, followed by some low-level cursing.

Doctor Reid strained to see who was there.

'I heard your nephew's having a few issues, Ainsley,' she said. 'Elijah, isn't it? Would you like me to have a chat with him while we're here?'

Ainsley shook her head and gestured over her shoulder at Balgair. 'Not right now.'

Doctor Reid leaned in towards Ainsley, their heads almost touching. 'Magoria Jepp is still at the Tolbooth, and she mentioned a visit.'

Ainsley blanched. '*Inquisitor* Jepp? What's she still doing here?'

'She wasn't convinced by Oddvar's explanation of what happened in the vaults, the psychic disruption, and it feels like there's more to it than a simple investigation, especially now the girls are back. We need to get rid of her before all our secrets come tumbling out.'

Delores saw them both switch their attention to Prudence. Prudence shifted her weight from foot to foot but said nothing.

'I could have a quick look at Elijah,' said Doctor Reid, 'see if there's anything I can do before Magoria finds any more excuses to make everyone's lives difficult.'

Ainsley shook her head. 'He's a bit out of sorts, that's all. It's his Gift with the cutting and stitching that keeps him here. Haven't seen anything like it, but Balgair … well you know how he is. And we get very little sense from Elijah's mother, so no change there.'

Doctor Reid stifled a laugh. 'Valentina still spending all her energy talking to the ones the other side of the veil?' she asked.

Delores' ears pricked up at the mention of the veil. The dead they were talking about had crossed over, accepted their deaths, not like the reluctant ghouls that hung around Delores, the ones who wanted to claw their way back to a more physical existence.

Balgair rattled the paper pattern. Again. 'Lad's a creepy wee waste o'space if you ask me.'

'Well then,' chirped Ainsley, 'it's as well no one did ask you, Balgair Cormican.'

She placed her hand on Prudence's back and guided her towards a rail of coats and jackets. Prudence winced and arched away from Ainsley's touch. She looked at Delores. Her eyes were watery and her smile unconvincing, but she still managed a weak, 'Later, loser.'

Delores gave a sarcastic salute then slid her hand over the rail of trousers, feeling the different fabrics, until she found one pair that her hand instinctively lingered over. She tried to check the size but there was no label, so she held the deep aubergine-coloured trousers against her hip. She hoped to attract Ainsley's or Doctor Reid's eye, but they were focused on Prudence and her painful shoulder blades. Doctor Reid was holding a coat against Prudence's back. It was long and expertly tailored in deep velveteen red, a higher-status, jacked-up version of the coat she already owned. Prudence removed the silk scarf from her hair and swapped it for a black one, freeing the wayward feathery tufts that had developed over the summer. Her sleek brown bobbed hair was gone for good, and she would soon be something else.

Something Delores didn't understand. She could find the legends and the histories in the books at the Tolbooth, but no one wanted to talk to her about the reality of shapeshifting and what it would mean to Prudence, how she would live with the nuts and bolts of how it worked.

Delores folded the trousers back over their hanger. If they didn't want to involve her, she could at least offer some support. As she turned to go, the hairs on the back of her neck stood away from her skin like pins and she felt the shift in air pressure that heralded the presence of the dead. A Bòcan was close by, she was sure of it. But there was something else. Anxious mutterings interspersed with the odd sob were coming from an adjoining room at the back of the shop.

As her eyes adjusted to the dark corners, Delores could make out a thin boy, shorter, younger than her, with thick black hair swept back from his face. It had to be Elijah, Balgair's creepy *wee waste o'space.* Delores had endured years of being called creepy by Normals but to be called that by your own family was unimaginable.

And something was off. She could feel it now in the pit of her stomach: a churning, dragging sensation, greedily pulling at her own life-force. The boy was not alone in the dark.

Elijah took a few unsteady steps out of his corner and reached for the velvet curtain of a changing cubicle. He clutched the fabric to steady himself, never taking his eyes off Delores.

A three-bar electric fire next to the changing cubicle buzzed as Delores got closer, but the air around her was bitterly cold. If a Bòcan was close, why couldn't she see it? The Bòcain didn't hide from Delores. They were always keen to make her acquaintance.

Elijah shrunk back into the shadows, holding his hands up in front of him. 'Don't come any closer.'

'There's something in here with us,' whispered Delores.

Elijah nodded slowly, then flinched as Delores stepped towards him. She could see his sharp green eyes were brimmed with tears and blue-black underneath from lack of sleep. He wore the same white shirt as Gabriel, but under a waistcoat that was just a little too big, and jeans that sagged at the ankles of his battered black Converse. Where his sleeve was pulled back, greying bandages wound up to his elbow and looked silver against his brown skin. He looked past Delores, searching for Ainsley.

'She's with Doctor Reid,' said Delores. 'The doctor could look at your arm though. She's great with mystical afflictions.' Elijah flinched at the word *mystical*.

‘And normal stuff,’ Delores added, ‘not that … I mean … like Normal-normal just not…’

Elijah pulled his arm across his chest and Delores thought it really was time to shut up.

‘I just want it to go away,’ whispered Elijah.

‘Honestly,’ said Delores, ‘Doctor Reid’s lovely.’ She blushed as the word *lovely* was left hanging awkwardly in the air between them. She made a mental note to cringe about it later.

Elijah’s eyes flicked past Delores to the doctor, then back again. He tugged at the bandage and made a slender gap in the folds so he could slide his fingers inside and rake at the skin beneath. ‘Not this. *It.* I want *it* to go away.’ Elijah looked over his shoulder into the darkness.

His voice dropped to a whisper, ‘Are you the necromancer? The one they’re all talking about?’

‘I suppose so … yeah. I’m Delores. Why, who’s talking about me?’

Elijah looked at her puzzled. ‘The dead. Don’t you hear them?’

Delores hesitated, unsure how much Elijah could know about her. ‘Which dead?’ seemed a safe question.

Elijah shrugged. ‘Ones saying you can bring the dead back across. *They* want to come back now.’

Delores looked to check Balgair wasn't listening. She stepped closer to Elijah. 'You heard that?'

He looked into the dark again, sobbing and raking at his skin.

'You need help.' Delores tried to get Doctor Reid's attention without attracting Balgair's. She cursed her singular Gift; a bit of telepathy would be so handy right now. She was about to call out to her when Elijah stopped crying.

Delores felt another pressure shift.

She looked around her, checking every shadow, every corner. The Bòcan had moved closer. 'Where is it, Elijah? Why won't it show itself?'

Elijah spoke, his voice low and soft, drawing Delores closer until she could feel his breath on her cheek.

'It was cross because I wasn't strong enough. But it isn't cross now. It wants to play tig … it says you're it.'

Elijah grabbed Delores' arm so tightly that she could feel his fingers amongst her sinews and bones. She tried to pull away, dragging Elijah to one side as a shock ran up her arm and bright lights flashed in front of them, but Elijah kept hold as the room dropped away from them.

From deep inside the bright lights, Delores saw the dark shape of what once could have been a man. It was broad shouldered from the back, wearing a long leather coat with the collar turned up past its neck. One of the reluctant dead. A Bòcan.

Turn, turn, turn, thought Delores. If she could see its face, maybe she'd know what she was dealing with, what it wanted. As if hearing her thoughts, the figure slowly turned its head towards her, but the top half of its face was covered by a black mask that had a long beak-like nose. It was decorated around the eye sockets with feathers and small, black stones that glimmered in the lights. Through the mask, ice-blue eyes were watching her. The rest of its face was still unformed, a grey blur, and as Delores turned her head to try to gather more detail at the edge of her vision the fumes from the heaters gave way to smells of pungent rosemary and soothing lavender mixed with the prickly, cooling moth-ball scent of camphor. Smells she was familiar with. Smells that took her back to Senga Pennyroyal's pagan altar on Harris and her dead-end lessons on magikal healing. All except one. A bitter-edged smell that she could taste on the back of her tongue as she breathed.

The Bòcan stepped towards Delores, details of its hair sharpening then quickly fading; thick curls on top, short at the side, red one moment, swirling grey the next. She tried to step back as it held out a curled fist, but she still couldn't get free from Elijah's piercing grip.

As the Bòcan moved closer, it turned its hand palm upwards and uncurled its bone-white fingers, fingers that were tipped with narrow nails painted glossy black. Small brightly coloured petals fluttered from its hand to the floor. When its palm was fully open, the Bòcan bent and sighed a long rasping breath. The remaining petals lifted like snowflakes and brushed Delores' cheeks before falling, some catching on the rough texture of her coat, some landing softly on her tongue as she gasped then swallowed.

Delores closed her eyes. She focused her attention on pushing the Bòcan away, back to where it came from, away from the living world. 'This is my domain,' she said, slowly forming the words of her mantra. She drew on the energy kept deep in the pit of her stomach. 'I decide who shall pass. You are uninvited.'

The marks on Delores' neck grew achingly cold and she sensed a gentle creep across the surface of her skin as the end of one of the fronds curled back on itself. She felt like she was on the edge of a precipice, about to be overwhelmed. The pain from Elijah's grip made it hard to focus on forcing the dead thing back. She pulled at his fingers with her free hand, the pain in her tendons and bones lifting just enough for her to give one last push. Delores felt the reversal as the Bòcan stepped back into the shadows. Then she was falling.

Elijah let go and Delores hit the floor. Hard.

Delores could hear Ainsley shouting Elijah's name as a door slammed shut in the distance. She felt a hand land softly on her arm, another slipping under her shoulder as Doctor Reid helped her up. The floor felt like it was rising and falling in waves beneath Delores' feet. After a second or two, the room and the people in it pulled themselves back into focus. Prudence's face loomed closer to her than the others, eyes wide and unblinking, brimming with concern. She was saying something, but the words were muffled and non-sensical.

Prudence held on to Delores while Ainsley packed each purchase in violet-scented tissue paper that trembled as she worked. Balgair took his coat down from its hanger, hitched it over his shoulders and buttoned it with angry precision before announcing that he'd go find *the glaikit wee wretch.*

Doctor Reid placed her hand on Ainsley's, stopping her work for a moment. 'Tell me what's going on with Elijah. I might be able to help him.'

Ainsley pulled away and filled the awkward silence by commenting on each item as it was packed.

Prudence said nothing at first. She gripped Delores' hand tightly, as if letting go would send her friend hurtling off into the unknown, but Delores was numb, even to Prudence's vice-like fingers. A gnawing emptiness had settled deep inside her chest. She could think, but she tried not to. When she did, she saw flashes of the Bòcan slowly turning, its mask silhouetted against a bright light. She focused on staying upright even though she couldn't fully feel her legs.

Ainsley wrapped the last purchase, a white, high-collared shirt embroidered with delicate daisies. Delores focused on the pattern to keep her mind closed to whatever was hiding in the dark recesses of the shop, but the daisies swayed in front of her eyes, bringing waves of nausea with them. Ainsley placed the package on top of a second bag and turned her attention to Delores.

'Elijah's a good boy,' she said. 'I'm sure he didn't mean to hurt you. He wouldn't hurt anyone.'

Prudence squeezed Delores' hand even tighter. 'Funny how people say that after someone they *think* they know does something wicked,' she said. 'I'm sure Inquisitor Jepp—'

'Prudence!' said Doctor Reid. 'Apologise immediately. The last thing we need is to be arguing amongst ourselves! None of us fully understand what happened yet. Elijah is a Cormican and the Cormicans are our friends. Even Balgair.'

'Well, what *I* know,' said Prudence, 'is that one minute Delores was fine, or as fine as she ever is, next thing she's screaming and Elijah's throwing her to the floor. And something *awful* was in there with them. I saw it in her thoughts after she fell.'

'Stop it Prudence, please,' mumbled Delores. 'I just want to get out of here.'

'I'm sure there's an explanation,' said Doctor Reid. 'Let me know if there's anything I can do when you find Elijah.'

Ainsley put her head down and whispered, 'Thank you. I'm really...'

Delores, Prudence and Doctor Reid didn't hear the end of the apology. They were already out of the door and heading back towards the Tolbooth, all thoughts of afternoon tea at the Caledonian left scattered on the floor of Cormican, Bunsby and Cavalletto.

8

Doctor Reid tried to hail a taxi but the only driver that stopped drove off again when he caught sight of Delores' sallow face. Doctor Reid put her arm around her, and although the spinning nausea didn't stop Delores felt lighter. As they headed back to the Tolbooth, Prudence walked three steps in front, making sure the crowds parted. Delores wasn't sure if she'd done it by glaring or by psychic manipulation, but she was grateful either way. Every step was an effort and it felt like an eternity before they were standing outside the Tavern next to the Tolbooth.

Doctor Reid propped Delores against the wall and helped Prudence look for her key. The Tavern Bòcan was in his usual spot, peering in through the window at the drinkers inside. Delores was used to him by now. He'd never tried to take anything from her, so she wasn't anxious around him, though she did feel the cold spreading from his body. She'd often wondered about giving him a name, trying to find out who he was and why he was so reluctant to pass through to the peaceful oblivion of the settled dead.

Delores took some deep breaths, hoping it would steady her nausea and stop the pavement roiling beneath her feet. She closed her eyes and the world steadied.

'Did Prudence find her key?' she asked. 'I really need to sit down.' But all she could hear was tutting and the rustling of packages in bags.

She opened one eye. Maybe she should ask the Bòcan its name, distract herself. She knew she was vulnerable after what had happened at Cormican's but at least something positive might come out of the day. 'Hey,' she said, expecting it to turn and face her.

The Bòcan tilted its head.

'Yeah, you,' said Delores, 'the guy always looking in the window. What's your name?'

As the Bòcan turned towards her voice, there was nothing. Its eyes were deep, dark pools, its features grey and unformed except for its slack jaw hanging in an exaggerated gawp. Slowly it turned back to its eternal task of gazing through the window, as if Delores wasn't there at all.

Gabriel was sitting cross-legged on the floor, knitting a set of cuffs to protect Bartleby's skin from his shackles. One cuff was already in place and Bartleby was admiring its rainbow pattern when Prudence and Ernaline burst through the door, holding Delores up between them.

Gabriel dropped what he was doing and jumped up.

'What did you do to her this time, Pru?' he asked.

'I didn't do anything. And if you ever call me *Pru* again, I'll make sure there's something nasty prowling around your dreams.'

Gabriel put his hands up. 'I'm joking! What happened?'

'We're not sure,' said Doctor Reid, 'except that it was an extreme paranormal event. Did Magoria react in any way? I did wonder if she'd sense something was amiss.'

'Haven't seen her,' said Gabriel. 'She was busy searching through Oddvar's room for something and then she scurried off upstairs with a stock ledger from the back room.'

'Let's hope it's gone unnoticed then,' said Ernaline. 'We need to get Delores up to bed without attracting any attention.'

'I am here, you know,' said Delores. She pulled away from Doctor Reid and took the bag of sherbet straws from her pocket. Bartleby sniffed the air and came as close as his chains allowed. Gabriel took the bag and handed it to him.

'Merci, ma petite cochinelle,' grumbled Bartleby. He sniffed the air again.

'What?' asked Delores.

Bartleby bit the top from one of the sherbet straws and spat the end of it onto the floor. He stuck out his long, pointed tongue, poured the blue sherbet along it and smacked the dissolving sherbet against the roof of his mouth. He shuddered. 'Ce n'est rien, ma petite. It is nothing. But maybe … maybe … no, it cannot be that. I am mistaken.' He shrugged before retreating inside his dark space, taking the sherbet straws and the knitting with him.

Prudence sniffed Delores' hair. 'You do smell a bit weird.'

'Cheers,' mumbled Delores.

It was Doctor Reid's turn to sniff. 'Moth balls?' she said. 'How bizarre.'

Delores felt she might die of shame. 'Can you just get me to my room?'

'Good idea,' said Doctor Reid. 'Take my place here, Gabriel, and I'll do my best to distract Magoria with our purchases.'

As Prudence handed over the bags, Doctor Reid

took a small bottle from her pocket, whispering, 'Just two drops in the morning for the pain and here's my card; address is on the back if you need me.' Prudence slipped the gifts into her own pocket as Doctor Reid gave her a warning look. 'Think of a truth about the bottle in case Magoria sees it as a secret in your mind. It wouldn't take much to connect the dots all the way back to shapeshifting. It's the ambergris. Only works on shifters, so she'll know.'

Prudence caught Delores watching but instead of an expected *mind your own* business, she held Delores closer.

When they reached the dining room, Magoria was in the chair opposite Oddvar, using the light from the fire to read a document. Doctor Reid positioned herself in front of Magoria as the others stumbled past. It looked as if they were going to reach safety when the toe of Delores' boot touched the troll cross scratched into the floor outside Gabriel's door.

Delores felt an intense pain in her stomach as waves of nausea swirled through her body, sharper than they'd been at Cormican's. She felt her knees buckle and Gabriel and Prudence lowered her to the floor as she started to wretch.

'Oh no, not here,' whispered Prudence. 'She'll hear you! You'll never protect yourself in this state!'

Gabriel rubbed Delores' back. 'Can you get up?' He looked over his shoulder to the dining room. 'Prudence is right, you've got to move.'

Prudence pulled at Delores' arm, trying to get her up, but Delores couldn't move past the troll cross. The charm was supposed to stop the dead, not the living, though right now Delores wasn't sure which she'd rather be. The nausea spread from the top of her head to the soles of her feet. Even her toes felt sick.

Doctor Reid's super-loud chatter was bouncing around the vaulted ceiling as she told Magoria how busy the streets were, how charming Ainsley had been, how splendid Prudence looked in her new coat. But something else was buzzing in Delores' ears. At first, she thought Doctor Reid's diversion was failing, that Magoria was searching inside her brain, looking for clues, but as the sensation intensified. Delores knew she was destined for one place only – vomit central. She put her hand over her mouth to stop it, praying Prudence wouldn't get splattered. Sweat bloomed on the back of her neck, trickling in rivulets down under her shirt collar and along the tentatively curling fronds of her hidden marks.

'Get back,' she gurgled through her fingers.

'Don't you dare,' Prudence hissed.

Delores' cheeks billowed. Prudence edged back.

One final wretch and it was all over.

But there was no splatter.

As Delores pulled her hand away, a rainbow of dried flower petals fluttered to the floor. The air filled with the same scent of camphor, lavender and pungent rosemary that heralded the arrival of the terrifying Bòcan at Cormican's. A bitter unidentified tang at the back of Delores' throat fizzled to nothing and the seething nausea was replaced with angry hunger-rumbles. She looked up at Prudence, waiting for an equally explosive reaction.

Prudence mumbled, 'Gross,' but in a tone more curious than disgusted. She took a pair of white gloves from her pocket and put them on, never once taking her eyes from the petals. She scraped the floor with one hand, scooping some of them into the palm of the other.

'What. In all-Hell. Are you doing?' whispered Delores, spitting out more dried petals between each word.

Prudence peeled her glove back over the petals in her palm, making an odd little bag of it. She dangled it in front of Delores' face. 'Research.'

'We've got to move,' said Gabriel. 'Doctor Reid's running out of conversation.'

Delores touched the troll cross with the toe of her

boot but felt nothing untoward. She stepped lightly over it as Gabriel shoved the rest of the petals to one side with his foot.

As the door to the stairwell clunked shut behind them, Delores, Prudence and Gabriel heard Magoria yelling, 'For Heaven's sake, Ernaline, stop babbling, you're worse than that wretched gargoyle!'

9

It was dark when Delores woke. She'd been dreaming about Bartleby, all alone in his sanctuary. She reached into her bedside cabinet and searched for the powerful cream-coloured chess piece he'd given her in the spring, the funny little soldier biting his shield. She found it quickly and ran her hand over the carved details around its back. She'd take it back to Bartleby so he wouldn't think they'd abandoned him.

Delores could hear Prudence's snuffling deep-sleep breath and assumed dinner had been and gone. A bowl of cloud-shaped cookies topped with swirls of white and silver icing had been placed on her bedside table alongside a small tartan flask with a white cup doubling as a lid. Delores devoured the lemon-scented, butter-rich cookies, washed down with chocolate just hot enough to gently burn the back of her throat. Her stomach demanded more. She pulled a jumper over her pyjamas, picked up the empty flask and bowl, and slipped the chess piece into her pocket.

Delores crept past Magoria's room, hoping it was still early enough for her to be sound asleep.

The fire in the dining hall was still blazing and Oddvar was exactly as he'd been left, his face deathly pale in the firelight. Gabriel was sleeping at his feet, fully clothed. Delores placed her hand on Oddvar's and whispered, 'Please come back to us, Uncle.' There was no response, but she noticed the tendrils were getting thicker around his wrists. She wondered how long he could stay like this, if he would ever recover. As she bent to tuck Oddvar's blanket more tightly around his slender legs, she noticed a scattering of drawings under Gabriel's arm, and an ink pen poking out from beneath his hand. She tentatively slid one of the drawings, no bigger than a postcard, from under his sleeve. The paper was gossamer thin, so fragile that Delores was afraid it might disintegrate. She held it to the light of the fire. It was an intricate drawing of a moth, detailed and breathtakingly beautiful. The light from the fire glowed golden through the paper, filling the spaces between the lines with tones of amber, copper and warm orange. It accentuated the pattern on the moth's forewings and the delicate lines that joined to form what looked like a human skull on its thorax. The drawing was intoxicating and though she didn't quite understand why, Delores felt compelled to take it. She folded the paper with great reverence and tucked it into the pocket of her pyjamas next to Bartleby's chess piece.

Delores tiptoed to the kitchen but didn't dare turn on the light. Still exhausted, she'd be extra vulnerable to Magoria's questioning if she woke her. There was enough light coming through the window to find a small pan. She poured a generous amount of milk into it and set it on the range to heat up, warming her hands as she waited.

She wiggled her toes inside the thick woollen socks she always wore in bed, happy to be snug, feeling safe and relaxed in Cook's domain, but still listening intently for Magoria's door opening. Her ears prickled in the silence. She wondered why it was so quiet. There was always some distant city noise, no matter what time it was, but the air felt soft and thick. The hairs at the base of her skull prickled. Something had moved closer, but the room was empty.

Delores glanced over her shoulder then laughed quietly to herself. All she saw was the pale streetlights through the kitchen window that looked out over the service steps. She turned back to the pan. There were a few bubbles forming in the centre of the milk. Not long now and she could scurry back to bed. She shifted from foot to foot as cold began to seep through her socks.

Milk, she thought, *focus on the milk,* but the more she tried to ignore it, the greater the feeling grew that something was watching her.

There was a sharp tap-tap-tap on the window.

Delores could hear her own breaths as she scanned the room for something stirring amongst the shadows, then thought of the troll cross that she'd drawn by the shop door. Nothing should get past that.

'Focus, Mackenzie,' she whispered. The milk was bubbling in the silken silence, but there was no sound of it hissing against the hot metal.

There was another sharp tap-tap-tap on the window. Quicker this time.

The feeling of eyes peering at the back of her neck shifted from vague unease to deep discomfort and the frost markings on her skin ached as her feet turned to blocks of ice inside her socks.

Delores told herself it was a bird at the window. That she was just cold. That it was autumn and the Tolbooth building was ancient.

Tap-tap-tap turned to scratch, screech, scrape.

Slowly, she spun round, the wool of her socks

snagging against the rough floor. A shadow moved across the window, partially blocking the light from the street.

Delores' breath grew visible in the kitchen air and above the sweetness of burning milk, she could smell camphor, lavender and rosemary. The nausea came stampeding back.

The tapping stopped and Delores held her breath as a hand pressed against the outside of the window, its palm and fingertips solid, then the side of a face, a beakish outline, the shell-like curve of an ear, listening. The Bòcan had found her, and it was gaining form.

'Not now, you creeper,' muttered Delores. The last thing she needed was Magoria waking up in the middle of a visit from the reluctant dead. That would raise far too many questions and Delores might not have the strength to hide the truthful answers. She gathered the energy she needed from deep in the pit of her stomach. She visualised it travelling up the front of her spine to her brain, pushing forward, pushing away the Bòcan that lurked on the steps outside. There was a moment of resistance, then the Bòcan slipped away from the window and into the night. It had made its point. It might not be able to get in, but it would be outside, waiting, somewhere in the darkness of the Old Town. Delores didn't feel sick anymore, but there was an empty space deep inside her, like a tiny part of her had been hollowed out. As her fingers drifted over a new marking curling along her collar bone, she wondered if the nausea was the only thing the Bòcan had taken away with it.

The distant city hum pushed its way back through the muffled silence and the milk hissed against the top of the range as it boiled over. Delores pulled her cuff down over her hand and dragged the hot pan and its burning milk from the range. It clattered into the sink, and she froze for a second, heart pounding as she listened for Magoria.

Reassured she was completely alone, Delores cleaned up the mess, wondering what the Bòcan wanted with her. *Same as all of them,* she supposed. If that were true it would be back, and she couldn't stay inside the Tolbooth forever.

When she was done, Delores noticed a plate of cookies just along from the stove top and, next to that, a small red bowl of her favourite chocolate-covered cherries. She swore they hadn't been there before. She popped one of the cherries in her mouth, crunching through the dark chocolate shell to the sharp sweetness underneath. She took another and then picked up one of the cookies. These cookies were not for her. The icing on the round buttery thins was sprinkled with sparkling crystals of blue sherbet. Delores knew exactly who they were for.

'Thanks, Cook,' she whispered, aware of a shadow disappearing from the kitchen followed by the sound of steps shuffling along the hall.

Delores finished her cherries, then crept towards the stairs. She took one last reassuring look over her shoulder as she went down the darkened stairwell, hand against the wall, towards the shop at the front. She followed the sound of Bartleby's snoring and placed the chess piece and the plate of cookies on the floor at the edge of his sanctuary.

As she walked away, a fragile voice called after her in the dark, '*Merci bien*, my little ladybird.' As Delores turned, she saw Bartleby's manacled hand reach out for the plate and her heart broke just a little bit more for him.

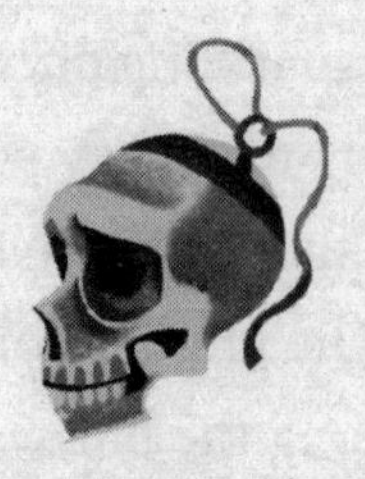

10

Magoria was wickedly gleeful. Not only had she found something *interesting* amongst Oddvar's things, but she'd also had an invitation from the First Minister to attend their official residence for morning coffee. Delores found it hard to imagine Magoria's clicky little fingers wrapped around anything other than the peculiar eggs she was so obsessed with, but she was glad of the chance to escape her scrutiny for a while. It also gave them the perfect opportunity to visit Doctor Reid.

Prudence was super-keen on the idea of a visit. Her adoration of the good doctor was getting embarrassing. Delores looked away as Prudence carefully packaged the strange petals from her vomiting episode in an envelope and mumbled something about asking Doctor Reid for further help with the emergent feather tips. Prudence was wearing her new clothes from Cormican's, moving more comfortably in the super-soft daisy covered shirt, swishing around in her ankle-length tweed skirt that was cringingly like Doctor Reid's and easing into her long fitted coat. Her boots, as Ainsley had predicted, looked glorious. Prudence was certainly eye-catching, but this was Edinburgh Old Town; people would glance, admire and look away. They would write her off as an eccentric, a young academic or someone playing a role at one of the historic attractions. If they didn't look too closely. Delores pulled on her own boots over her vintage tweed trousers and waggled her feet around to better admire the effect. Today might just be a better day. Today they'd find a way to help Oddvar, to get everything back to normal, and Doctor Reid was exactly the person they needed to speak to.

Before slipping it into her pocket, Prudence showed Delores the clear glass bottle with a silver stopper that Doctor Reid had passed to her. It had a tiny dosing cup attached to its neck by a silver chain and as Prudence tipped it from side to side, a bubble worked its way from the base up through the oily amber liquid. It was small enough to fit easily in Prudence's hand. 'Oil of ambergris from the Faroe Islands apparently.'

Delores moved closer. 'Looks vile.'

'It's not that bad. Tastes OK. It's mixed with honey and a few other things.'

'Is it helping?'

Prudence nodded. 'A little with the pain but the feathers are still there, a bit more obvious each morning. I … I think I'm running out of time.' Delores waited for Prudence's tediously slow blink. But it didn't come. Instead, she saw an almost translucent flash of white across her friend's golden eyes, that quickly retracted. She tried a reassuring smile, but Prudence knew that Delores had seen it. They didn't just need answers about Oddvar. They needed to work out how to get rid of Magoria before she extracted the secrets that would finish them all, secrets that would see them dragged to the prisons of the North. Crucially, they had to do it before Prudence fully shifted for the first time into her other form. If that happened, they were all done for, perhaps even Doctor Reid for being an accomplice.

Delores put the drawing of the moth in her coat pocket whilst Prudence adjusted her new black scarf to cover any stray baby feathers at the base of her skull. Delores decided she would ask Gabriel about the pictures once they got him outside the shop, away from Magoria's attentions.

They almost succeeded. Gabriel brushed his hair, put on his glasses, even got as far as the door but, once he looked out into the street, he changed his mind. 'I think I should stay with Oddvar,' he said, 'and I can sneak some breakfast to Bartleby once *she's* out of the way.' There was a rumble of agreement from Bartleby's dark sanctuary.

Delores didn't need psychic abilities to know that there was more to it than that. 'Magoria's off on a jolly with the First Minister, remember? Plus, she's massively distracted by something or other. We could easy slip Bartleby some food and all go together.'

'There must be a reason she's like that,' said Gabriel, 'and it can't just be coffee with the First Minister. We all know Normals aren't *that* fascinating, not even the top ones. And she didn't try to get any truths out of me at breakfast. How about you?'

Delores shook her head. There had been a slight feeling of pressure, an urge to tell Magoria about the figure at window, but that urge had disappeared when Magoria triumphantly informed them of her invitation.

Prudence shrugged. 'No, nothing now you mention it.'

'Exactly,' said Gabriel. 'She's up to something.' He looked out into the street again, pulling his glasses back up to their usual perch on the top of his head. When a passer-by glanced at him, he looked down at his feet, avoiding the stranger's curiosity until they walked on.

Delores put her hand on his arm. 'Are you sure that's all it is?'

Gabriel nodded and stepped back into the safety of the shop. 'I'll sit with Uncle Oddvar. Read to him.'

'He'll like that,' said Prudence. 'Be careful, though. Just because Magoria's all Little Miss Sunshine, it doesn't mean she's above a psychic ambush.'

As Gabriel turned to go, Delores remembered the drawing. It was a risk, but she hoped Magoria was too busy pawing at whatever she'd found amongst Oddvar's belongings to pay them much attention.

'How do you do them?' she asked.

Gabriel looked at her, puzzled.

'What now?' huffed Prudence. 'We need to get going.'

Delores unfolded the drawing. 'I know your eyes are getting worse Gabriel and I know you can't see well enough to do something like this. And it's so beautiful.'

Prudence took the drawing from Delores, barely stifling a gasp. Delores was almost overcome with the desire to snatch it back again, but she didn't want to risk the delicate paper.

Gabriel blushed and his scalp shone pink through

his white hair. 'I don't need to see well to do that. I touched Oddvar's hand so I could get a glimpse of the moth again. I thought it might be a clue to getting rid of Magoria. I put the pen on the paper, closed my eyes and let it happen. I can see the drawing super-clear when I'm doing it, but when it's finished, not so great. Maybe it's part of my divination. Who knows? I'll ask Oddvar when…' He looked at the ground, hands thrust deep in his coat pocket. 'You should have asked before you took it.'

'I know,' said Delores. 'I'm sorry. Can we take it to show Doctor Reid? She might know something about the moth.'

Gabriel nodded and disappeared back into the darker recesses of the Book Store. Delores knew he'd be heading straight back to Oddvar's side.

'You might have mentioned the drawing,' said Prudence. 'We are supposed to be in this together.'

Delores was about to reply when a van screeched to a halt next to them, bumping the curb and parking half on the pavement. She was so busy trying to think of an excuse to give Prudence, that she didn't pay the van any more attention until two men in blue boiler suits, woolly hats and thick, gauntlet-style gloves flung its back doors open. They dragged out a crate marked *Caution: Dangerous Creature Containment* and let it crash onto the pavement. Delores and Prudence jumped back to avoid the men as they dragged the crate to the shop door.

'You've got the wrong address,' said Prudence. 'There aren't any animals in there.'

The shorter of the two men kept his head bent over the crate, grunting as they tried to manoeuvre it closer to the step. 'Good news,' he said, 'since we are not looking for animals. Are we, Guillemot?'

His companion chuckled and then tapped the side of his nose. 'Indeed we are not, Bombina, indeed we are not.'

'We have not got the time for whatever this is,' said Prudence, tugging on Delores' coat sleeve.

'It's just a bookshop,' said Delores to the men as Prudence pulled her away. 'And it's closed. Good luck by the way, finding the dangerous creature thing.'

Prudence took Doctor Reid's card from her pocket and flashed it in front of Delores' eyes. 'Ladystairs Close here we come,' she said, as she marched off up the Royal Mile.

Delores looked back over her shoulder as she started after Prudence. She'd expected to see the men dragging the crate away again, heaving it back into the van, but the shorter one was banging hard on the door of the Book Store.

'All-Heaven's sake!' shouted Prudence. 'Let Magoria deal with them. We're wasting time.'

Constantly being two steps behind Prudence in the race to get Doctor Reid's attention was getting tedious. Delores understood the fascination, she just wished Prudence was less obvious about it. Her hand drifted to the drawing of the moth in her pocket, and for a fleeting moment she understood that feeling of hypnotic enchantment, but as Delores struggled to connect the two things, Prudence was already disappearing into the morning crowds ahead of them.

11

The Writers' Museum could have been plucked straight from the pages of a fairy-tale, dropped down to rule over the taller, more rigid buildings that surrounded Ladystairs Close. Delores had no problem imagining Doctor Reid living there. She looked up at its domed tower and high balcony, watching for a friendly face at a window, but Prudence had no patience for waiting. She marched up to a young museum attendant who was polishing the wooden doors and gave him Ernaline's calling card. 'We're expected,' she said. She smoothed her coat then checked the edges of her scarf with nimble fingers.

The attendant shook his head and handed the card back. 'No one of that name here. There's a medical centre down in Stockbridge if you need a doctor.'

He stared hard at them both, his cobalt eyes unblinking from beneath his thick dark-auburn fringe. Delores felt a dark chasm blooming in her chest, as if some disaster was about to engulf the cobbled square, taking everyone with it. She grabbed Prudence's arm and stepped backwards.

'Really, Mackenzie?' said Prudence. 'You fell for that? He's one of us.' She turned back to the attendant. 'Don't be a bore…' She tilted his name badge upwards '…Findo. We all know she's not *that* kind of doctor.'

Findo tutted and went back to his polishing. The sensation that had been building up behind Delores' ribcage fizzled to nothing. The words *rookie* and *error* screamed in her head.

'Up to the very top of the spiral stairs on your right as you go in,' said Findo. 'There's a step ladder leading to a trap door.'

There was no doubt that the ambergris was working its wonders on Prudence. She rushed up three flights of stairs, leaving Delores in her wake. As Findo had told them, the staircase came to an abrupt halt at the foot of a stepladder. Prudence stood on the bottom step and rapped three times on the trap door. There was a brief pause, then the rattling of a bolt. The trap door creaked open, and Doctor Reid was staring down at them. 'Girls! Come up!'

Delores and Prudence clambered up the ladder. Doctor Reid held out her hand and hoisted them up into the apartment, clanging the trap door shut behind them.

The walls inside the tower room were painted a warm deep ochre. There was another set of stepladders on the left with a fluffy towel and a pair of bed socks folded neatly on the bottom rung. Tucked away under the ladder was a writing desk and a chair with a hot-water bottle where the writer's feet would rest. Every bit of available wall space above the desk was covered in shelves crammed with jars of remedies and specimens, tiny sets of scales and impossibly dainty spoons. It was all lit golden by a flood of light from the balcony window at the other end of the room. Opposite the desk was a bookcase carved with the same angels and cherubs that graced the shelves in the Tolbooth dining room. Their wings pressed against the ceiling as if to stop it from falling.

If Delores could design her dream home, this would be it. She wandered over to the bookshelves, taking it all in, but Doctor Reid's books were slightly less to her taste. They were hard-working texts with crinkled spines and faded covers, books about anatomy, botany and zoology, about cures and Paranormal maladies. Little space had been left for fiction; just half a shelf, a third of the way down. Delores pulled out a copy of *Wuthering Heights.*

'Borrow it if you like,' said Doctor Reid. 'I do love it, but it's a strange tale.'

Delores smiled as she slid the book back into its place. 'Not all that strange, seeing ghosts at windows.'

'Hmm. Sorry about Findo, by the way,' said Doctor Reid. 'He looks out for me, and I was worried Magoria might drop by unannounced.'

Prudence answered from behind her. There was a hard edge to her voice, 'Do we look like a pair of Magorias? And if you're so worried about her, why's he here?'

Delores followed Prudence's steely glare towards a fire that blazed fiercely in a small black stove near the entrance. Next to it, snuggled deep in a chair and wrapped up to his eyes in a blanket, was Elijah Cormican.

Prudence took off her coat in silence and draped it carefully across the back of another soft armchair near the fire. She made a point of dragging the chair away from Elijah before she sat down.

Doctor Reid touched Prudence's shoulder. 'Elijah could do with some friends, don't you think?'

Prudence looked down at her lap and Delores could tell she was struggling between her fury with Elijah and her desire to please Doctor Reid. Prudence nodded, but still glared at Elijah every chance she got.

'Now,' said Doctor Reid, 'what can I get for you? I have a grand range of medicinal teas.' Doctor Reid made her way over to the apothecary shelves.

Delores and Prudence shook their heads, grimacing. 'No thanks,' they chimed in hurried unison.

'Ah yes,' said Doctor Reid, 'the Witches of Harris. I'm sure you've had enough curative tea this summer to last a lifetime. I'm told they can't pass a clump of something or other without steeping it in hot water and calling it blessed!'

Prudence blushed and hung her head.

'Oh, I'm sure they're lovely people,' added Doctor Reid, blushing in return.

Elijah drained a cup he had on his lap and shuddered as he put it on the floor next to him. Delores offered him a sympathetic smile, but he looked away. He tucked himself into the folds of the blanket, like he was trying to disappear amongst its stitching.

'Hot lemonade then?' asked Doctor Reid. She took a big jug of fresh lemonade and a chunky mug of sugar from her desk and tipped them into a kettle already warming on the top of the little stove. She placed four mismatched mugs next to the pan to warm, gestured for Delores to take a seat near the fire and perched herself on the arm of Prudence's chair. Prudence relaxed back into the cushions once Doctor Reid had made her choice of seats, sighing triumphantly as she warmed her toes.

Doctor Reid smiled at Prudence. 'Glad the tincture's working,' she said. 'You mastered that step ladder like an athlete! Just be careful with the dose. The ambergris and honey are fine, but the extract of devil's claw packs a punch. Right, let's get to the bottom of what happened at Cormican's. Elijah, tell the girls what you told me.'

Elijah pulled his blanket down just enough to make himself heard. 'I told Delores some of it already, didn't I?'

'Only a bit,' said Delores, 'and you were really upset.'

Elijah took a breath. 'OK, so I didn't know the whispering was dead people at first.'

'Here we go,' sighed Prudence, 'more spooks and ghouls.'

'Hey,' snapped Delores, 'I don't tread on your toes so how about we keep the ghoul comments down?'

'They asked me to tell my mum some stuff, who to pass it on to,' said Elijah. 'She told me what the whispering was and then I started helping at her séances, passing messages on. Only when she was a bit stuck though. And it made Dad happy to think *she* was doing it. I never meant…'

Prudence tutted, stopping Elijah mid-sentence. Doctor Reid put her hand on Prudence's shoulder and nodded for Elijah to continue.

'It was just messages from the settled dead at first. Mum called them that and said it was harmless, 'cos they were happy. But then I started to hear the others, the unhappy ones.'

'The Bòcain,' whispered Delores, 'that's what *my* mum calls them.'

Elijah nodded. 'They kept talking about a girl called *Delores Mackenzie*, and how she brought *little Maud* back from the other side.'

Delores was horrified. 'That's not what happened!' She turned to Doctor Reid. 'If Magoria hears that, I'm done for. Maud wasn't properly dead, I swear.' But for the first time, Delores felt a fluttering of doubt.

Elijah sat forward in his chair, letting his blanket fall. Delores noticed that the bandages on his arm had been replaced with a soft gauze and there was the shimmer of ointment around their edges. He pulled his sleeve down when he caught her looking. 'I haven't told anyone else,' he said. 'Not even Auntie Ainsley, I promise.'

'I'm sure the girls believe you,' said Doctor Reid. 'Isn't that right, girls?'

Delores nodded, but Prudence sat stony faced.

Doctor Reid tried to break the awkwardness by pouring them all mugs of piping hot lemonade.

'Don't worry, Delores,' said Doctor Reid. 'Oddvar filled me in on your particular Gift before he withdrew himself. I know the danger you're in if Magoria discovers the true depths of your necromancy, but she's not allowed to question me. That's why we thought Elijah would be safe here. I'm not under investigation. Not yet anyway.'

Doctor Reid handed a lemonade to Elijah and whispered, 'Continue, sweet boy.'

Elijah wrapped his hands around his mug. 'There was a big séance,' he said. 'Like massive. There'd been a lot of messages coming through and they were all kind of the same, about a dangerous man but none of them would say his name. Said to warn their families though. The dead can't be scared, can they?'

Prudence and Doctor Reid looked at Delores for answers.

'They can be all kinds of things,' said Delores, 'just like the living. Anything else?'

'They just kept saying he was back. Mum knew who some of them were. She said they'd died of grief after their special Gifts were stolen. Mum said one was a siren, but I don't know about the others.'

Doctor Reid's mug hit the floor. 'Sorry!' she said,

flustered. 'I don't know what got into me.' She jumped up and grabbed a towel from next to the stove and threw it over the spilled drink. 'You didn't tell me that bit before, Elijah,' she whispered. 'Were they all women?'

Elijah nodded. 'Five of them I think.'

'Five?' Delores asked. 'You sure?'

Elijah hesitated for a moment. 'I think so, but it all went a bit mad, and the whispers got muddled. I never saw them though, not ever, but when it all went quiet there was something at the back of the room, in the dark. And a weird smell. I thought it'd go away after the séance, but it didn't. I knew it was in my room at night, watching me. Then all the rooms. Then outside, right up behind me. I got *so* tired, and I stopped hearing the other dead and Mum got worried 'cos we couldn't do the séance and we needed the money and Dad was getting cross … then you came to the shop. It told me it'd leave me alone if I just…' Elijah's jaw trembled as a tear slid down his cheek, 'played a game of tig.'

'And I was it,' whispered Delores.

12

The spectre of what Elijah had told them hung heavy in the air.

Delores was the first to speak. 'I saw it … him. When Elijah grabbed me,' she said.

Elijah pulled his blanket back up below his eyes, glancing around the room, searching the darker corners.

'Don't worry,' said Delores. 'He's not here now.'

'Sorry to push this,' said Doctor Reid, 'but it could be important. Was there anything unusual about this … this creature?'

Delores nodded. 'He was hard to see at first, they are until they gain a bit of strength, and there was a whole load of flashing lights and dramatics to deal with, but he was wearing some kind of mask over the top half of his face. And I was scared. That's not normal for me. Elijah's right about the funky smell as well. It wasn't normal dead-smell.'

Prudence choked on her lemonade. 'There's a *normal* dead smell?'

Delores shrugged. 'Well … duh? Some of them do smell but most of them don't, but this filled my head until I couldn't think about anything else. I couldn't push it back to the dead like Oddvar taught me. Next thing I knew, you were picking me up off the floor.'

'And then she vomited these up when we tried to get her to bed.' Prudence handed the petals to Doctor Reid in the envelope. Delores felt sick again. The thought of vomiting all over Ernaline Reid's apartment was beyond mortifying. She put her hand to her mouth just in case.

'Have you got a dry biscuit?' she asked.

Doctor Reid shook her head apologetically. She opened the envelope and took a close look at the petals inside. Delores could see her hand shaking as she took a few of them between her thumb and first finger and held them up to the stream of morning light coming in through the balcony window. 'What was the smell, Delores? At Cormican's?'

Delores gagged. She took a sip of the lemonade, pleased to feel the burn on her tongue, the hit of sugar and the sharp tang that made the memory of the smell less real. 'It was camphor, I think, maybe rosemary, and some lavender. There was a sharp edge to it though, something I didn't recognise. I think that's what made me black out.'

Doctor Reid's mood was growing graver with every question. 'There is another plant amongst these petals. Something I'm not familiar with, but I think Elijah must be allergic to it. It could be what made him itch so much, especially if he hadn't been in contact with it before. This … dead thing, was there anything else you can remember? Anything about its face?'

Delores closed her eyes and tried to picture the figure looming at her out of the dark at Cormican's. 'Not much. The mask was in the way. Red hair though, curly, cut short at the sides.'

Doctor Reid turned her head slowly to look at Delores. 'And the mask?'

'Like one of those doctors you see in stuff about the plague,' said Delores. 'But that doesn't feel right. It didn't feel that old. More like a carnival mask, black with feathers and a beak.' She shuddered thinking of those bone-white fingers unfurling, scattering the petals. 'Oh, and painted nails,' she said. 'Glossy black, really narrow. Bit like Oddvar's come to think of it.'

Doctor Reid put the envelope of petals in her skirt pocket and crossed over to the bookshelf. She ran her finger along the spines of books below her meagre selection of fiction before pulling out a heavy volume that she bundled up in her arms. She gestured for Delores and Prudence to join her at her writing desk. Elijah cast off his blanket to follow behind.

Doctor Reid dropped the book onto her desk.

'I haven't looked at this in ages,' she said. 'A lot of it is nonsense and idle tittle-tattle. A historian friend gave it to me, thought I might find it amusing. There's something about the petals that stirred a memory, that and what Elijah said about Gifts being stolen from Paranormals.' She looked at their expectant faces. 'Don't look so serious. It was a story made up of hysteria and gossip, I'm sure.'

Delores was not convinced, and by the look that flashed across Prudence's face, neither was she.

The book was filled with paper clippings, most of them yellowed. There were columns of script with faces peering out of the spaces next to them, all in black and white. The edges of clippings fluttered as Doctor Reid turned the pages towards the back. She moved swiftly through reports of banshees in the early eighteen hundreds in the Little Ireland area of the Old Town, to demons taking over St Giles' Cathedral for *a short but entertaining* period in 1904 and an incursion of rebellious witches in 1926. Delores was about to ask if there was anything in there about her parents when Doctor Reid found the article she was looking for in the middle of the 1980s. She brought a lamp closer to the page and ushered Elijah forward. He slipped in front of Delores, and she caught a whiff of camphor from his hair. She wondered if she smelled the same.

There were three articles glued to the page, all with the face of the same man looking out at them. In the first he was young and clean shaven, his curls falling forward over his face, the sides cut short, not dissimilar to Delores'. The next was a graduation picture, taken in front of a building topped with spires and gargoyles: he was standing alone, grim-faced as the world went on around him. The third photograph showed him at a party wearing a white, stiff-looking, high-collared shirt and a fitted tweed suit. His eyes glared at the camera through a black feathered mask; a mask that came out over his nose like a beak. Revellers danced behind him, dressed for a carnival, raising glasses to each other, their heads thrown back laughing. Hanging around the man's neck was a silver skull on a chain, about the size of a golf ball. He was holding it up to the camera lens with a look that Delores couldn't quite place, but it made her squirm. The first two photographs were labelled *Hartigan Fox,* the last announced *The Fall of Doctor Death.*

Delores ran her hand over the third photograph and whispered, 'That's him.'

Prudence sighed. 'Doctor Death? Really? Isn't this just some old tabloid nonsense?'

They all looked at Doctor Reid, waiting for an answer.

'Maybe,' she said, closing the book before Delores had chance to read any of the article. 'I wasn't in Edinburgh in the 80s. York I think, or was it Bergen?' She tucked the envelope of petals inside the pages. 'I'll check the story with my historian friend before we give it any further consideration, find out why Hartigan Fox really became known as *Doctor Death*. It seems possible that you are being followed by the remains of a very sinister individual, Delores, so be watchful. You too, Prudence.

She reached out and touched Prudence's arm, and Prudence glowed brighter than the table lamp.

'All-Heaven save us,' muttered Delores as Doctor Reid ushered them all back to their seats.

The paper clippings had brought a deep chill into everyone's bones, and they needed the heat from the stove to help gather their thoughts.

Doctor Reid topped up their drinks, and when she got to Delores she paused, 'Have you seen this creature since Cormican's?'

Delores nodded.

'And you never thought to mention it?' shrieked Prudence.

'Uhm, I'm mentioning it now?' said Delores. 'You're not always in the mood to listen, and we are currently kinda focused on getting rid of Magoria.'

Prudence glared at her, then folded her arms tightly across her chest and flung herself back in her chair.

That must have hurt thought Delores, but before she could ask Doctor Reid interrupted.

'Did the creature speak to you?'

'No. I just saw it through a window at the Tolbooth last night.' She felt another rush of nausea and that deeper pit of exhaustion blooming again, more intense than she normally felt after an encounter with a Bòcan; this bled through to the marrow of her bones. 'I really need to eat something,' she whispered.

Doctor Reid was immediately by her side, placing a cool hand on her forehead and checking her pulse. 'You are pale, and your lips are a bit blue. Have you swallowed any more of the petals?'

'No,' said Delores. 'I just need rest. And sugar. Sugar helps a lot.'

Doctor Reid took a white paper bag out of her pocket and handed it to Delores. 'Keep sucking on these. It'll help the sickness as well as giving you an energy boost.'

The bag was tied with the same black and white string Esme had used on Bartleby's sherbet straws. 'You go to Esme's?'

'Of course,' said Doctor Reid. 'Esme's a good person. You can trust her.'

'But she's…' Delores knew that sentence was not going to end well. She opened the paper bag and tucked a barley sugar twist inside her cheek.

'What?' said Doctor Reid. 'A Normal? That doesn't mean she can't be trusted. Esme sees a lot from that little shop, even if she doesn't *really* see it. And there's something almost magical about her treats, don't you think?' She peered at Delores. 'I am concerned about the effect this creature is having on you though. I rarely see someone so pale who is still up on their feet and walking around.'

'I wish I could say the same,' said Delores, as thoughts of Hartigan Fox and what it could all possibly mean came rushing back in alongside the hit of sugar and sweet barley.

13

Doctor Reid tried to lift the sombre mood by humming to herself as she collected everyone's mugs. Prudence's eyes stayed firmly on her as she crossed the room and leaned her back against the far end of the bookcase. There was a creak as the carved angels released themselves from the ceiling and half of the shelves spun slowly on an axis to reveal a small kitchen behind them. Delores nudged Prudence's foot with her own just as Doctor Reid turned round and caught her.

Prudence blushed as she desperately searched for a reason to be staring. 'What about the moth picture?' she blurted.

Delores was already unfolding it. She gave Prudence a look that said *getting to it, genius!*

'What moth picture?' Doctor Reid came quickly to Delores' side again, wiping her hands on her skirt.

She looked over Delores' shoulder and breathed in sharply. 'That is beautiful. May I have it?'

'*Have* it?' both girls said.

It was Doctor Reid's turn to look embarrassed. 'I didn't mean to *keep* it.' She laughed as she said it, her hand dancing around her throat.

Delores reluctantly handed over the delicate piece of paper. She knew exactly what Doctor Reid had meant. She felt the same way.

'Hold it up to the light from the fire, then you'll really see how beautiful it is,' said Delores.

Elijah knelt up in his chair to get a better look.

Doctor Reid opened the small door of the stove to expose the flames. Their light gave the moth life again, turning its wings amber and emphasising the shape of the skull on its thorax.

'Acherontia atropos,' whispered Doctor Reid. 'Death's-head hawk moth. Why do you have this?'

'Gabriel made it,' Delores said as she reached for the paper.

Doctor Reid pulled back just a little before handing it over. 'Gabriel? Well, looks like we have ourselves another...'

'Another what?' asked Prudence.

Doctor Reid thought for a moment, looking at both girls carefully then changing her mind about what she was to say next. 'Is this the only one, Delores?'

Delores shook her head. 'He's done lots of them. If he tries to read Uncle Oddvar's future, this is what he finds, ever since Oddvar and Magoria had that big fight. We're hoping it's a clue to getting rid of Magoria before she gets what she needs to call a Gathering.'

'Oddvar's directing us towards another Uncle,' said Doctor Reid. 'He's one of the few in the history of our society to retire. He has these moth markings on his skin.'

Delores lightly touched her collar bone through her shirt, her fingers hovering over the new frond that had curled there since the Bòcan had found her in the night. 'Are markings a bad thing?' she asked.

'No, they're not *bad*,' said Prudence, rolling her eyes. 'A lot of Old Ones have them. How can you not know this stuff? Didn't your parents tell you anything?'

'Oh, and you've got such great parents?'

'Harsh,' Prudence mumbled. She turned away, but Delores knew she'd still be hanging on Doctor Reid's every word.

'They are often connections to nature,' said Doctor Reid. 'Oddvar has … a little of the *insect* about him? His posture, his colour?' Doctor Reid unfastened the pearl buttons of her high collar and dropped her shirt a little down the back of her shoulders. 'You might want to see this too, Prudence. It may even change the way you feel about your situation with the feathers. I'm sure it all intersects in some way. And you, Elijah? I don't mind.'

Elijah shook his head and retreated under his blanket, leaving just his eyes and his hair peeping out over the top.

Across Doctor Reid's shoulder blades and up to the base of her neck were the coloured markings of butterfly wings. The tones were muted with a subtle iridescence, the same powdery look Delores had already noticed.

'Lepidoptera,' whispered Delores, feeling the word flutter freely in her mouth. The markings were a rich deep brown towards the centre, spreading to orange patches with eye spots towards the edges of the wings.

'Scotch argus butterfly to be precise,' said Doctor Reid, covering it up again. 'Started to appear when I was fourteen.' She looked intently at Delores, waiting. The passing seconds felt like agony until finally Delores nodded.

'Great,' said Prudence. 'More secrets.'

Delores couldn't figure out if Prudence was hurt or angry. 'I wasn't ready to tell anyone and they're not like that, they're not moths or butterflies or insects. It's private.'

Doctor Reid put her arm around Delores' shoulder. 'Whenever you're ready, I'll take a look. We can figure out what it means together.'

This time, Prudence's emotions were completely transparent. 'Can we bring this back to Gabriel and *his* moth please?' she snapped. 'Who's this retired Uncle?'

'Obsidian,' said Doctor Reid softly, as if saying the name might conjure him from the air. 'Obsidian Strange. He lives at the grace of the King in an apartment at Holyrood Palace.'

Both girls reached immediately for their coats.

'Tread carefully,' said Doctor Reid. 'Obsidian and Oddvar had a serious disagreement years ago.'

Delores and Prudence waited to hear more, wide-eyed. 'What about?' Prudence finally asked.

Doctor Reid looked at Prudence, her eyes flickering to the point of a feather escaping below her scarf. 'It's not important,' she said. 'Just be on your guard. Oddvar must be desperate if he wants Obsidian Strange involved.'

Delores buttoned her coat. 'And if we can get rid of Magoria, we can get Uncle Oddvar well again. I really could do with his help with this Hartigan Fox creep.'

After an agonising pause that begged for reassurances, Doctor Reid simply said, 'Don't ask for Obsidian directly, or you'll be sent away by palace security. Look for a small oil painting of the moth in Gabriel's drawing. It's by another Gabriel: Gabriel Dante Rossetti. Three super gentle knocks on the space beneath the painting should do the trick. I'll let you know about the petals and newspaper clippings once my research is concluded.'

14

Prudence marched off ahead while Delores used her blue chalk to draw a troll cross on the underside of the trap door that led to Doctor Reid's apartment, quickly muttering the words of her mantra. The troll cross would be safe there, Findo might wipe one away from the front door, and it should keep any roaming dead away from Elijah while she was gone.

Prudence was already halfway down the Royal Mile by the time Delores caught up with her. She could tell by Prudence's rigid back and clenched fists that she was in a fury and all attempts at peace-making proved futile. Prudence stomped off ahead along the crowded pavements, only slowing to a stop when they reached the side gate of Holyrood Palace, where she stood seething with rage. Then she whipped round to face Delores, backfooting her, forcing her to step away. As unthinkable as it was, Prudence looked like she might cry.

'How could you?' said Prudence. 'I told you all about my…' she looked over Delores' shoulder and then behind her '…*feather issues*. That one secret alone could get me caught up in a Gathering, get me sent away to rot in some jail. But you? You kept something *so* huge from me. I could have gone looking in your brain for stuff, but I didn't because I thought we were friends. I thought … oh forget it.' She turned back to look through the gates.

Delores was stunned. All this time she had wanted her almost-friend back, and she'd been there all along, waiting for her.

'I'm sorry,' said Delores. She reached for Prudence's arm. 'You were dealing with a lot already. I thought I'd wait 'til we got back, tell Oddvar, and when I knew what it was all about then—'

'Oh great. Feel free to move me further down the list. You know what, Mackenzie? When you're making things worse, just … stop!'

Delores knew she'd messed up, but Prudence wasn't totally blameless; forever pushing Delores away with her sharp comments and put-downs.

'How are we going to get in?' said Delores, trying to bring some calm to the situation.

'Oh, do me a favour,' snapped Prudence as she stomped off towards the ticket kiosk.

Delores took a moment to calm herself. She put one of Doctor Reid's barley twists in her mouth and waited for the sugar burst to take the edge off her exhaustion. Fudge would have been better, quicker, but these did help quell the nausea. She watched from the gate as Prudence parted the queue of visitors waiting for their tickets, smoothing the sides of her coat, ready to cast an illusion over an unsuspecting ticket seller. Prudence was many things and one of those things was being extremely useful in the absence of cash.

The hairs on the back of Delores' neck prickled. She scanned the open courtyard, looking for signs of a Bòcan, hoping it wasn't Hartigan Fox. She was still reeling from their last encounter. She stepped into the courtyard and looked towards the archway where Prudence was busy convincing the ticket seller that she really should let them through.

Amongst the living souls that weaved in and out of the tables and chairs on the café terrace, one figure stood alone, hands by its sides. Its head was tipped forward and dark eyes looked up from under a heavy fringe. The edges of the figure were frayed and faded to a silver shimmer below its ankles. It gave the Bòcan the appearance of floating, something Delores hadn't seen before. Drawn in by her own curiosity and the overwhelming chasm of sadness oozing outwards from the Bòcan, Delores stepped towards it.

The Bòcan didn't move as the crowds milled around. Each living person stepping to the side or behind it at the last moment. When Delores was just a metre or so away, she could make out a camera hanging around its neck. The camera was expensive looking, heavy, but the lens was shattered. It looked like a young woman, not fully an adult, but close. Delores turned her head to the side and the details sharpened. She could make out faded jeans and a grungy looking T-shirt but nothing more than that. Delores moved closer, expecting the Bòcan to reach out to her. She was learning to deal with angry ghouls, but the pure sad ones? They were tough on her emotions.

The Bòcan looked up, as if only just aware she was standing there. Delores wanted to help; this was more like the Bòcain that used to come to her when she was small. It made her think of home and her parents. Part of her knew that she was being drawn in, but she didn't care; she wanted that feeling back, the one where she was doing something right for a change. But the Bòcan stared straight past her, as if she wasn't there. Delores could hear a winnowing, pleading sound, the words *I'm lost, help me* fading in and out, but the Bòcan made no attempt to take anything from her.

As Delores reached out to touch its arm, its outline scattered as it evanesced into the hubbub of the crowd. It was like some kind of switch had been flipped and Delores was somehow unseen, but she didn't know how or why. Her wondering was shattered by Prudence stampeding into her head, flashing an image of tickets at her and a demand to get over to the archway before she messed everything up. As usual.

Inside the palace, Delores trailed behind Prudence as she marched up a grand wooden staircase carpeted in blue. The walls were covered in tapestries and paintings that Delores assumed were of royalty or nobility or whatever it was the Normals called them. Thankfully, the only painting they needed to recognise was the one of the moth.

Prudence dodged in and out of the other visitors, scanning the walls and the doors before moving swiftly on. The rooms smelled of polish, dust and too many souls – living and otherwise. Delores had her guard up. She was sure to attract unwelcome ghoulish attention in a place with such a long and bloody history. But there was nothing, and that nothing was making her nervous. She caught glimpses of shadows out of the corner of her eye, but when she tried to look more closely, they slipped away through walls and behind tapestries. One slid into a harpsicord painted with golden birds and flowers, tinkling the keys as it disappeared. Distracted by the shadows' lack of interest in her, Delores walked smack-bang into Prudence.

Prudence had stopped at the foot of a four-poster bed draped in heavy red fabric. If looks could kill, Delores would have been joining that shadow amongst the strings and keys of that golden harpsicord.

Prudence pointed at a dark wooden door off to the left of the bed. In the centre of it was a small painting in a dull-bronze, lightly carved frame. It was different from the other paintings they'd seen, unremarkable in a way, and the only one on a door rather than a wall. Prudence stepped over the guard wire, signalling for Delores to follow.

Close up, the painting was simply awesome. A death's-head hawk moth painted against a background of scrolling purple leaves, its wings vibrant against the contrasting colour. The signature was tiny, but they could make out a D, a G and an R looping around each other at the start of it and then squiggling out into something that might have said Rossetti.

‘Has to be it,’ whispered Delores.

Prudence stood guard, capably confuddling anyone who might challenge why they were by the door, and not the other side of the guard wire where they should be. Delores knocked the prescribed three times just below the picture frame, so softly that her skin barely brushed the wood. There was a subtle purring of well-oiled clockwork and the door clicked open a slither.

A voice from inside said, ‘Enter quickly and close the door behind you.’

Obsidian Strange was standing next to an elaborate cabinet decorated with two glossy red hearts. He was facing away from them, hands clasped tightly behind his back. He’d carefully positioned himself to the side of a mirror so that he could observe them, but they could not properly see him. He was wearing the familiar tailored trousers and buttoned boots of an Uncle, but his jacket was glossier and split into a long tailcoat that grazed the back of his knees. His black hair came over the top of his high shirt collar and was scooped into a small bun at the base of his neck. He rolled his broad shoulders backwards, puffing himself up to seem taller than he was.

Obsidian turned his head slightly to the side, but not enough for them to get a good look at his face.

His shadow crept across the room until its head was almost touching Delores and Prudence's feet. 'Please be seated,' he said. He kept his hands firmly together as his shadow gestured towards two heavily embroidered chairs placed side by side in front of a spindly table. The table was set for afternoon tea, though it was barely past 11.

As they sat, the shadow crept back, waiting.

Delores mouthed *say something* at Prudence.

The shadow tilted its head, listening. Delores didn't want to take her eyes off it; she didn't trust how it moved independently of its master. She put her hand on the drawing in her pocket in case the shadow had light fingers.

Prudence cleared her throat. 'Uncle Oddvar…'

'You're students of Oddvar? If only you had said to begin with.'

Prudence frowned. 'But that's exactly what I began with.'

'Get out,' growled Obsidian. His shadow stretched behind Delores towards the door. There was a click followed by the sound of it creaking open.

'Please,' said Delores, panicked. 'Just hear us out. Oddvar's sick and we don't know if he'll ever get better.' After several seconds, she heard the door click shut again, and the shadow moved closer to its master.

'Continue,' said Obsidian, his voice a quarter-tone softer. The shadow reached up onto the table and pushed an unfeasibly small teacup towards Delores. Prudence kept her hands in her lap as Delores reached for the teapot and poured a few drops of steaming silver-grey liquid into the cup. She thought about taking a sip, but the teacup's handle was so tiny she would have had to pinch the thing between her fingers. 'We have an Inquisitor at the Tolbooth,' she said.

'I know all about the Inquisition. Every Paranormal in Edinburgh knows.' Obsidian stifled a yawn. 'Brought on by you I believe, and your … *adventures* … with the dead of this city. Tell me something more interesting and I might let you stay.'

'There was an argument,' said Delores. 'Oddvar put himself into some weird cocoon phase. He's getting taken over by wispy creeping tendril things.' Obsidian bristled at Delores' description. 'I don't know what else to call them,' she added.

'They are elemental threads.' He sounded annoyed, irritated.

'Uhm, OK,' said Delores. 'He's weaving himself into a cocoon with elemental threads?'

Obsidian nodded. 'Extreme measures. Most likely fatal if the situation is prolonged. He must think a great deal of you to protect your secrets in such a mortal fashion.'

The word *fatal* hovered in the air. Delores and Prudence kept their focus on Obsidian. Catching each other's eye would make that word real.

The shadow gestured at some delicate finger sandwiches on a scallop-edged plate. Delores lifted the plate, and the floral scent of wild honey flooded her senses. Delicate edges of purple and yellow flower petals peeped from between the soft white bread. Oddvar's favourites were also Obsidian's. Delores offered the plate to Prudence.

'For you only, Necromancer,' snapped Obsidian. 'Not the shapeshifter.' He shuddered at the word.

Prudence looked down at her lap, mortified and Delores saw a small tear drop onto her beautiful new coat. She put the plate of sandwiches back on the table and pushed her teacup away. The shadow reared up in mock outrage and Obsidian turned to face them fully at last, chuckling to himself. He had mischievous eyes so dark they looked black, and a miserly, tight-jawed grin. Subtle markings of a death's-head hawk moth crept from the back of his neck to his lower jaw, the same oranges and ambers of the picture that had glowed so beautifully in the firelight. Where Doctor Reid wore her mothy iridescence well, Obsidian Strange carried his darkly.

‘Kinship,’ said Obsidian through gritted teeth. ‘Admirable.’ This time, the shadow pushed two teacups forward. Delores was ready to swipe the wretched cups from the table when Prudence took up the teapot with a shaky hand and poured a few drops of her own.

‘That wasn’t very nice of you, *Uncle* Obsidian,’ said Delores, ‘and Prudence isn’t *just* a shifter, she’s a gifted illusionist and—’

Obsidian’s grin vanished. ‘Get to the point or leave.’

Delores knew to choose her next words carefully. Navigating Obsidian Strange was no easy task. ‘Gabriel,’ she said, ‘he’s a divinator…’

‘I know what he is.’ The shadow snatched back the plate of sandwiches and reached for the door again.

Delores took a deep breath. ‘Gabriel was able to see an image of a death’s-head hawk moth in Oddvar’s mind and draw it.’

Obsidian held out his actual hand and clicked his fingers. He wanted the moth picture. *Her* moth picture. Delores overcame her outrage and took it from her pocket. As she stepped towards Obsidian, Prudence reached for the hem of Delores’ coat and tried to pull her back, shaking her head, but Delores knew it was the only way they would get any further.

Obsidian took the picture as nimbly as a pickpocket. He smiled, refolded it and placed it in a small gold box on top of the cabinet. Devastation washed over Delores, a ridiculous sense of grief for a piece of paper she'd owned for less than twelve hours, if she'd ever owned it at all.

Obsidian grinned. 'I'm sure there are plenty more where this one came from. It would seem that your friend's secondary Gifts are taking shape, a beguiler perhaps.'

Prudence and Delores looked at each other, puzzled. Something Prudence didn't know about? A thought even more outrageous than the freely roaming shadow or the impossible teacups.

'I suggest you ask Doctor Reid about that particular Gift,' said Obsidian. 'She is one after all. You look confused. Have you not felt … enchanted by her company?'

Delores and Prudence both shrugged, but they met each other's side-eyed glances with a frown.

Obsidian sniggered. 'I thought as much. Ever wondered why everyone loves the boy? Why everyone positively craves Doctor Reid's company? They are beguilers. Verb: to beguile, charm or enchant, often in a deceptive way. It is one of the Gifts. It will become stronger as the boy gets older; even spread to the things he touches. A more pleasant aspect of our society if used well.' He homed in on Prudence's reaction. 'Don't worry, Shifter, not everyone is affected by it. Your feelings could be real. Oh, your blushes betray your confusion. Do I mean the boy? Or do I mean the doctor. Only you know the answer to that. And these feelings? They're probably the only genuine thing about you.'

Delores couldn't keep a lid on her anger. 'You're supposed to be an Uncle, a guardian, you have no right to be so cruel. And her name is Prudence!'

Obsidian rolled his eyes. 'Back to the matter in hand. Inquisitor Jepp must be getting close to your most dangerous secrets for Oddvar to take such extreme measures. Necromancy beyond acceptable limits I believe. Opening the boundary between the living and the dead, causing a rift in the Paranormal Sphere no less.' He wagged his finger at Delores. 'Naughty, naughty! And you *Prudence,* daughter of shapeshifting Solas Sigurdarson would be in mortal peril should you shift into your other form at a time as inconvenient as an Inquisition. Where is your...' Obsidian cleared his throat '... *father*?'

Prudence took a sip from her tiny cup, grimacing in a way that made Delores decline the shadow's offer of more from the teapot.

Prudence placed the cup back in its saucer, steadying one hand with the other as she returned it to the table. 'He'll be back, I know he will.'

Obsidian nodded slowly, his tongue sweeping his lips. 'Clever old Oddvar to seek my help. Magoria Jepp was a student at the Tolbooth many years ago when I was Uncle there. Gifted, but not as gifted as her sister, Agnes. When Agnes died, strange accidents befell any Inquisitor who came to solve the riddle of her death. It was all recorded, but the Jepp family are exceedingly powerful, and that record could somehow…' Obsidian took a deep breath '… not be found. It is no coincidence that Magoria Jepp returned to the Tolbooth when news reached Norway of a powerful necromancer studying there. Ask yourself what *Senior* Inquisitor Jepp is so afraid of, what has kept her here all summer long, searching the Tolbooth when one of her junior staff could have kept watch until your return, and why, oh *why* is she so determined to close the Tolbooth Book Store down?'

The shadow slithered back to the table. The teacups were pulled away and the teapot dragged with a screech towards the tower of cakes.

'That's quite a lot of questions,' said Delores. 'Any chance you could, you know, actually help us out?'

Obsidian turned back to look out of the window.

'Be wary, Necromancer. I hear one of the reluctant dead covets your attention.'

Delores shifted uneasily in her seat. 'What's that got to do with anything?'

'You think these things go unnoticed?' said Obsidian. 'There is chattering amongst the living and the dead. If I am aware of it, so is Magoria Jepp. You must be rid of it before something happens to strengthen the inquisitors' case.'

'Easy for you to say,' muttered Delores.

'This is not a game,' snarled Obsidian. 'The Paranormal Sphere is a delicate eco system and you and your *Gift* are tugging at its loose threads. If you allow another soul to cross back to the living, Magoria will have everything she needs. The High Council already considers us rebellious, who knows who this woman could take down alongside Oddvar and his wretched students.'

'That is NOT what happened,' shouted Delores. 'Maud was not fully dead!'

There was a pause as Delores' words echoed around the room. Even the shadow was still.

'Are you sure?' Obsidian's tone was low and silky.

Delores was aware of Prudence staring at her. She could feel her nudging at her mind, trying to get in. 'I'm sure,' she said, scowling at Prudence.

Obsidian nodded. 'Find Agnes Jepp, or what little is left of her. Use your Gift as it is intended, *speak* to Agnes, find out what happened all those years ago. She could be your key to getting rid of Magoria Jepp before Magoria Jepp gets rid of you. Now leave.'

'You've hardly helped at all,' said Delores. 'What about Oddvar? You said his condition was—'

'I also said LEAVE!' Obsidian turned with fury to Prudence. 'GET OUT!'

Prudence spoke low and even. 'You let Agnes down. They were both under your care, Agnes and Magoria. How dare you look down on me.'

'Prudence,' gasped Delores. 'Don't...'

Obsidian swiped the golden box from the top of the cabinet and his shadow reared up at Delores and Prudence like Frankenstein's monster. It spread itself across the table, scattering the tiny teacups, shattering one against the teapot. Delores jumped from her chair and scrambled towards the door. Prudence grabbed her arm as she passed.

'Ask him how we find this Agnes person,' she said. The shadow yanked at her chair, rocking it to the side, until Prudence was forced to stand.

'I don't need to. I already know where Agnes Jepp is,' said Delores, 'and so do you.'

As they made their way back to the Tolbooth, not a single Bòcan tried to catch Delores' attention. Even the simple ghosts were absent, but Delores felt something close behind her, almost stepping on the back of her boots. Each time she turned to check, there was nothing there, only a nauseatingly familiar smell in the air around her. She still had so many questions, but there was one thing Delores was sure of; she was going to need a bigger bag of barley twists. She popped one in her mouth and let it melt against her cheek as she chased after Prudence. Again.

15

Bartleby was gone.

Delores and Prudence stood speechless amongst the devastation. Bartleby's dark hiding place was scattered across the floor like shattered glass, and his blanket was lying trampled amongst the shards. A tacky grey fluid that Delores didn't even want to think about seeped from under his upturned basket. She reached into the space next to her and took Prudence's hand.

Prudence gave a squeeze of acknowledgement but didn't let go. '*She* did this,' said Prudence. 'It had to be her. And we *let* it happen.'

Still holding on, Delores knelt and lifted the edge of Bartleby's basket in the vain hope that he might be hiding under there. All she found was the rainbow knitting that Gabriel had given him, pulled from its needles, and a single blue sherbet straw.

Delores let go of Prudence's hand. She put her hands on her knees, drew in a breath that filled her lungs to their bases and she screamed. She screamed out her rage at her parents' disappearance, at the lies and deceit that followed, of their treatment at the hands of the Harris Witches, at Obsidian and at Solas for abandoning them, for poor Agnes Jepp, but most of all she screamed for their beloved Bartleby. And when she couldn't scream any more, she collapsed to the floor and sobbed.

Prudence knelt next to her. She placed her arm softly around Delores' back and rested her head against her neck until the sobbing stopped.

'We'll get her for this,' Prudence whispered. 'And she won't even see us coming.'

16

Delores and Prudence ran upstairs to find Gabriel. Instead, they found Magoria waiting for them, revelling in what she'd done. She must have heard the screams and Delores hated that she would have enjoyed every second. Sitting at the far end of the dining table, Magoria was puzzling over something in her hand. She didn't raise her head, despite their clattering arrival.

Oddvar was alone next to the fire. His book had slipped and was teetering at the edge of his knees.

Delores barely managed to hold Prudence back as she lunged at Magoria. 'What have you done with Bartleby?' she shouted. 'And where's Gabriel? He NEVER would have left Oddvar alone with *you*!'

Magoria grinned and tossed a small, cream object into the air, catching it again in her creepy alabaster hand.

Prudence shrugged Delores off and tilted her head, listening, clearly reaching out for Gabriel, opening her mind in the hope of a reply.

'Stop it,' urged Delores, terrified that Prudence's lapse in guarding would allow Magoria into her brain.

Prudence stared at Magoria. 'You locked him in his room? I *knew* he wouldn't just let Bartleby go.'

Magoria put the object she was toying with on the table, cupping her hand over it. 'The boy's room isn't locked anymore. His guilt is keeping him in there.'

They heard a door open, and Gabriel came wandering, bewildered, into the dining room. His face was waxy and his hand trembled as he pulled his glasses down from the top of his head to hide his puffy, red eyes. 'I tried to stop them,' he said, 'but they dragged me up here and *she* locked me in.'

Magoria sighed and gestured to the chairs around the table. 'Sit down. All of you.'

'You can't question us without Doctor Reid here,' said Delores. 'She's our Guardian in … in…'

'In Oddvar's absence,' Prudence added. For once, Delores was thankful to Prudence for finishing her sentence.

Magoria took her hand away from the object she'd been playing with. It was Bartleby's chess piece, the little soldier with the shield. 'I said *sit down*.'

Delores took the chair at the opposite end of the table; Gabriel took the seat nearest Oddvar and Prudence was on Delores' other side. As soon as she settled in her seat, Delores was flooded with the thought that she was unable to leave. She caught a glance between Prudence and Gabriel and knew they were all trapped.

Magoria slid the chess piece into the centre of the table and placed her index finger on top of it. 'Finding this in the demon's possession was such a gift. It's on a list of stolen artifacts, artifacts that the government of the Normals is quite rightly irate about. It was the final nail in his little stone coffin.' She punctuated her sentence with a grin.

Delores was cut through with guilt. She should have known Magoria would find it.

'Pity I have to return it,' said Magoria. 'The Normals have no clue as to its real power. Perhaps I could negotiate an amnesty, keep it for myself.' She kept her finger pressing into the top of the little soldier as he bit his shield and grimaced his accusations at Delores. Magoria flicked the figure over and it fell face down on the table. 'Of course, I don't *need* it. It's just additional proof. I have enough on Oddvar to get him dismissed and have this place closed for good.'

'You can't have,' said Gabriel. 'Even I can't see what Oddvar's thinking.'

'Even you?' sneered Magoria. She bent down to the sealskin bag propped against her chair. She stroked the skin lovingly with her hand before taking the brown Tolbooth Habitants ledger out and tossing it on the floor. Delores, Prudence and Gabriel winced as it landed, then waited as Magoria struggled to get a grip on a much weightier book. She swept her hand over the fine silver filigree that ran across its cover and round its spine. She held it to her chest, her nose against the forest-green edges of its pages, then inhaled, eyes closed.

Delores looked nervously across at Prudence to see if she recognised the book. Prudence knew all the stock, all the books that were for sale and those that were most definitely not.

Prudence shook her head, puzzled. Magoria clearly wanted one of them to ask about it. She opened her left eye, waiting.

Delores was the one to relent. 'What's—'

Magoria jumped in a little too quick. 'Evidence.' She sighed. 'It is evidence of *Egregious Misappropriation of Paranormal Artifacts*. A crime punishable with an extensive prison term, removal of all personal wealth, privileges and, of course, status.' There was the glimmer of a smirk with the last word.

Delores felt her shoulders drop from somewhere up around her ears, and even though she was still rooted to her chair, she felt relieved. This was going nowhere. Oddvar would never steal. 'You're wrong,' she said, looking at Prudence and Gabriel for backup, but they both kept their eyes on the table.

Magoria opened the ledger to a place marked with black ribbon. Her eyes scanned the page and then glanced back up at Delores. 'A highly valuable book is missing from the shop's most private inventory: *An Exalted Celebration of The Higher Order of Angels.* And then I find a receipt of exchange, hastily tucked at the back of this ledger, which, incidentally, had found its way into a secret little cupboard in Oddvar's room. A receipt for, and I quote…' Magoria pinched the frame of her glasses between her thumb and finger. '*The daemon that is Bartleby L'Aubespine, corporeal body and eternal damned soul in exchange for…* oh dear, that very same highly valuable book on the subject of angels, a book that was not Oddvar's to trade. So, *the daemon that is Bartleby* is on his way back to his old master in Paris, and Oddvar will face the High Council on charges of theft as soon as his crime is evidenced by the return of said book.'

'You can't do that to him,' said Delores. 'He's ill.'

Magoria looked over her glasses at Delores. 'Illness will not protect him. In fact, it could be argued that

Oddvar Losnedahl's self-inflicted *illness* is a thinly disguised attempt to evade justice. Not only a thief, but a coward. Oddvar will spend his final days in a prison cell. No food, no light … no books. That is, if the journey doesn't kill him first.'

'Uncle Oddvar is a good person,' hissed Prudence. 'Why are you doing this to him? Why do you even care about this place? About us?'

Magoria slammed the ledger shut. 'Oddvar is a delusional old fool and you wicked creatures have been allowed to run wild, to use your Gifts without boundaries or checks.'

'That's not true,' said Delores.

'Isn't it?' Magoria's face was as flinty as her voice. 'I've played along with your games for long enough,' she said. 'Offering me simple *truths,* taking me for a fool, yet all the while I watched glimmers of evidence, skulking behind your thoughts like shadows; evidence that I will carve out, evidence that will damn you all and close this wretched place for good.'

Magoria's rage sharpened with every word, pulling her body as taut as a fiddle string. She'd always been measured and cunning in her cruelty, but Delores feared Magoria was about to snap.

Magoria took the chess piece from under the ledger and looked at each of them in turn, first Prudence with her face set in defiance, moving swiftly past Delores to Gabriel. 'Maybe if I start with everyone's favourite Paranormal,' she said. 'You two will spill your secrets to save him. Oh, are you thinking I've seen all there is to see? A deeper, more cutting psychic journey into the boy's brain is sure to yield results. I'll try not to do too much damage.'

Delores was sick with fear that this was about to escalate to a whole new level of cruel. *Leave him alone* she thought, all attention to her own barriers against Magoria cast adrift.

As if the words had been spoken out loud, Magoria switched back to Delores and was inside her mind before she had the chance to protect herself. Delores felt Gabriel's trembling hand entwine in hers as she tried to force Magoria back out, but she was quickly overwhelmed by the sensation of cold, hard, clicky fingers wandering through her brain, pausing to scratch and probe and harvest. Magoria triggered memories that played out in Delores' head like a film: Oddvar's gentle questioning when Delores first arrived at the Tolbooth, how he had tried to get her to trust him, her growing love for Bartleby. Magoria ripped her way through those tender things, psychic cut by psychic cut, heading towards Delores' deepest most hidden secrets.

A starburst of pain erupted in the centre of Delores' brain. She needed to slow Magoria's progress, block her with something of value that wouldn't sink them all, and she had to do it before her defences were obliterated.

'I gave Bartleby the chess piece,' she blurted. She omitted to say that she gave him it *back*, but it was a tender enough morsel to derail Magoria; give Delores time to regather her mental barriers. There was instant relief as the pain sank from explosive to gnawing. Delores tried to focus on her breaths; she realised she was panting, and her mouth was bone dry. She looked at Prudence and Gabriel for reassurance, but the doubt and fear written across their faces said it all. Their futures, Oddvar's survival, the Tolbooth itself, was all resting on Delores' ability to keep Magoria out, and neither of them truly believed she could do it. That pain cut deeper than Magoria ever could.

Magoria puffed her cheeks out in frustration. 'I admire your quick thinking, but don't insult me with cheap diversions.' She clicked her fingers and the pain reignited like a match-strike. Delores couldn't focus. She had to keep Magoria away from her thoughts of Obsidian. If she saw that, she'd know they were onto a way to get rid of her. Obsidian's clue held the key to ridding them of Magoria, of ending the inquisition and any Gathering that might follow, Delores was sure of it.

Think. Think. Think.

The pain struck again. Magoria was back in her mind in a flash, leaving Delores no time to defend herself. There was a slicing pain deep inside her head, and a window into her most guarded memories was forced open. Thoughts began to tumble out: thoughts about Gabriel and his drawings, about Doctor Reid giving Prudence the medicine.

Medicine.

Medicine.

Medicine.

The thought screamed in her head and Magoria scooped it up.

'What *medicine*?' she purred.

Delores looked across at Prudence.

Wide-eyed and ghost-white, Prudence whispered, 'Please don't, not that.' Her mouth snapped shut at a second click of Magoria's fingers.

'I asked WHAT MEDICINE DID DOCTOR REID GIVE HER?'

Prudence squeezed Delores' other hand; her eyes filled with tears. Delores was unravelling. The more she tried to hide Prudence's secrets, the more she was leaving her own exposed. She felt them hovering, almost salty on her tongue, nudged forward by the growing pressure in her brain. She wouldn't do it; she couldn't do it. Delores would not sacrifice Prudence and the others to save herself.

'They're not simple ghosts,' she shouted. 'I don't just *talk* to the dead. The dead come looking for me. They know they're dead and they want … they want things.'

'Interesting,' said Magoria. 'Necromancy beyond acceptable practice. What *things* do they want?'

Delores could feel Prudence squeezing her hand tighter, begging her to stop, but the touch of Prudence's skin ignited an image of feathers in Delores' mind. She sensed Magoria's presence lurking, her attention prowling towards the feathers, towards evidence that could send her friend hurtling towards the prisons of the North. Delores was teetering and just as Magoria reached deeper for the truth about the feathers, the *real* truth, Delores blocked her with the thought of the Bòcan at Cormican's. She pictured it slowly turning with its bird mask silhouetted against the flashing lights. She thought of his tap-tap-tapping at the window. Magoria homed in on the memory of the face pressed against the glass, of petals falling from a bone-white hand. Then Maud. Poor Maud in the vaults, her spirit parted from her body until…

Magoria got to her feet and placed her hands on the table, leaning towards to Delores. 'What did you do?' she demanded. 'WHAT DID YOU DO?'

Delores' head throbbed as she frantically tried to put together a sentence that wouldn't condemn anyone but herself. 'It was all me. Oddvar didn't know I…'

There was a deafening crash of metal on stone. Prudence and Gabriel let go of Delores' hands as Magoria stepped briskly from her mind, furious at the interruption. There was another loud crash from the kitchen and an enormous copper cooking pot came hurtling through the kitchen door, followed by kettles and pans of varying sizes. The noise was ear shattering as it bounced from the stone floor to the high rafters, echo after metallic echo building into a crashing whirlwind as another utensil came flying out of the kitchen. Delores, Prudence and Gabriel covered their ears. Magoria shoved her chair from the table so hard it toppled backwards to the ground. The beautiful silver terrine was the next thing to hurtle through the door, then there was a moment of petrifying silence. Delores could feel a gentle thrumming beneath her feet as a rumbling sound built from somewhere deep in the kitchen, spreading across the whole of the Tolbooth. The rumble turned to a roar so base and guttural, it wouldn't have surprised Delores if the next thing to hurtle from the kitchen was a giant grizzly bear.

Magoria's face turned puce with rage and her deathly marble hands bunched into stony fists beneath her wispy cobweb cuffs. 'Cook!' she snarled. 'All-Hell take that damned creature!' She slammed her fists against the table and marched towards the kitchen. 'Enough of this outrage. I swear I will rip your mind to pieces from the inside!'

Delores was still trapped in her seat, and she could tell by their fidgeting that Prudence and Gabriel were as stuck as she was. Magoria was out of their heads, but she hadn't dismissed them.

'Do you think Cook will be alright?' whispered Gabriel.

'I don't know,' answered Delores. 'Oddvar told me Cook is super powerful so…'

They waited; eyes fixed on the kitchen door as Magoria slammed it shut behind her.

Something heavy crashed against the closed door and fell to the floor inside, followed by another long, painful howl and the sound of shattering glass. Then nothing.

Delores could hear her heart thudding in her chest, only just rising above the sounds of Prudence and Gabriel's rapid breaths. In the tortuous silence, Prudence cleared her throat and loosened her jaw, as if to check everything was functioning again. 'When Magoria shouted about the medicine,' Prudence whispered, 'I … I couldn't help it. A picture of the bottle of ambergris flashed across my mind. I don't know if she caught it but…'

The kitchen door creaked open and Magoria stepped back into the room. One of her sleeves was ripped at her shoulder and a long, lank strand of hair hung down over her face. She paused and straightened her spine, clicking her neck to one side. She approached the table slowly. She was trembling, Delores could tell from the vibrating strand of hair. Her eyes met Delores' and, as if suddenly aware of it, she tucked the offending strands behind her ear.

Delores felt lighter in her seat. 'Is Cook—'

'Go to your rooms,' snarled Magoria.

Delores stood but her legs were shaking. 'You're a monster,' she said. 'All Cook's ever done is care for us.'

'Oh really?' said Magoria. 'You know that for certain? I bet you've never even seen Cook,' she taunted, 'or you would question who the monster in the room truly is. You are testing my patience, Necromancer.'

Prudence and Gabriel stood slowly. Delores felt

Prudence place her hand gently on her shoulder. 'Come on,' said Prudence. 'Not yet.'

'Not yet?' repeated Magoria. 'You actually still think you can win? I've seen enough. I saw the rift in the Paranormal Sphere. I saw that little glass bottle with the ambergris, the bubble floating to the surface, its silver dosing cup. Only one person could have given you that. I know what you both are. And I know who I'll be taking down with you. Now go to your rooms.' Magoria took the brown ledger from the floor, a pen from her bag and sat down at the table to update her notes. 'Why are you still here?' she asked, sweeping her hand across a new page.

It was obvious there were no more words to be said. Gabriel tended to Oddvar, tucking his blanket back into place and adjusting his book so that it sat neatly under his hands. He turned his back to Magoria and curled defiantly at Oddvar's feet.

Prudence and Delores walked away in silence, and as Delores looked back over her shoulder the kitchen door clicked shut.

17

Prudence held the glass bottle of ambergris elixir up to the light. There was a couple of centimetres left in the bottom. She measured out a dose in the tiny silver cup and held it to her lips, but her jaw trembled as she tried to take a sip.

'It's not your fault,' said Delores. 'I'm the one who thought of the medicine and Magoria pounced on it. I am so sorry.'

Prudence pressed the silver cup against her lips and forced the tiny measure of her medicine down. 'It doesn't matter whose fault it is; the end result will be the same. She knows about my heritage and shapeshifting makes me an illegal Paranormal. My other skills will count for nothing. Add in what she knows about you, the dead and that whole paranormal rift thing and she has everything she needs. We're both heading north, and we know it. I just hope she doesn't have anything on Gabriel. He wouldn't survive. We'd lose both him and Oddvar.'

They sat in silence for a moment, their heads still pounding from the inquisition.

'Agnes,' said Delores. 'Obsidian said find Agnes, that she might be the key to getting rid of Magoria. Everything Obsidian said about her made sense in a mixed-up kind of way. He said she came *because* there was a powerful necromancer at the Tolbooth.'

Prudence raised her eyebrows at Delores.

'OK, OK, his words not mine, but think about it. If it was just the disturbance in the Paranormal Sphere they were investigating, she'd have left after she questioned Oddvar and Gabriel. Oddvar was super confident he'd be able to get through an inquisition and that we'd be able to come home safely. What if this isn't about Oddvar or how he runs the Tolbooth, or even about shapeshifting. What if it's about Agnes?'

'Agnes is dead,' said Prudence. 'Long dead by the sounds of it.'

Delores wondered what effect the ambergris elixir was having on Prudence's thought patterns. She was usually sharper than this.

'And who talks to the dead?' Delores turned her thumbs towards herself in a *this girl* gesture and immediately wished she hadn't. Prudence had no point of reference having been saved the torture that is High School for Normals. She looked at Delores as if she'd finally lost the plot. Feeling ridiculous, Delores dropped her hands to her knees. 'What if Magoria doesn't want to risk me talking to Agnes. What if *that* is what's she's so afraid of. What if…'

'… Agnes knows something that will sink Magoria?' Prudence looked like she was vaguely excited by the idea, but her shoulders soon dropped. 'Surely you're not the first necromancer to be here since Agnes died?'

Delores pushed all the parts of the puzzle around in her head and still it didn't all quite fit. 'Obsidian said that anyone who investigated had some kind of accident and I remember Oddvar wasn't too keen on having me here at first. Delilah said he'd taken some convincing. If Oddvar made sure no necromancers stayed here, for their own safety, Magoria would have no reason to come because…'

'…no one would be talking to Agnes.' Prudence thought for a moment. 'Maud saw ghosts though.'

'But what if she never told Oddvar? It wouldn't have been reported or added to the ledger. Her Gifts were only just developing so Oddvar might not have seen it, even if he did go looking. We all knew he was against talk of ghosts and now we know why.' Delores bounced off her bed and over to the clocktower door. She put her ear against it, hoping to hear something, anything, some indication that Agnes was there, just as Maud had told her. Agnes that didn't like the graveyard. Agnes, owner of the creepy dolls. Agnes. Jepp.

Delores waited, holding her breath, but there was nothing to hear from the other side of the door. 'Agnes,' she said. 'Agnes Jepp, are you there?'

Prudence snorted a half laugh behind her. 'You sound ridiculous.'

Delores waved her arm behind her, hushing at Prudence. 'I don't normally need to ask, OK? They normally come to me. Don't make it weirder than it already is.'

'Fine, but how many dead Agneses do you think are up there?' Prudence flopped onto her bed and Delores heard her swish her skirt under her as she settled onto her side, staring at Delores' back.

'Can you just keep quiet? I'm trying to focus.' Delores pressed her ear against the door. She thought she could hear some rustling on the other side of it, then gentle rapid breathing, like someone was struggling to catch enough air. Delores' skin tingled and the hairs on her neck did their usual thing. The wood against her ear grew achingly cold.

'Agnes,' she whispered.

A fragile voice started to sing a nursery rhyme on the other side of the door. Some of the words broke apart but Delores could make sense of most of it, piecing the breaks together as the song was softly repeated.

Where did you go to?
Where did you hide?
You're not in any wee places I tried.
No trace of footsteps,
No sight nor no sound
God rest you and keep you,
Deep down in the ground.

The singing faded on the final line and Delores heard footsteps retreating up the stairs of the clocktower, towards the clock mechanism.

'No! No! Agnes!' she shouted, banging on the door. 'Come back, I need to talk to you.' But there was nothing. The hairs on her neck rested against her skin; there was no prickling, no squirming sensation. Agnes, or what was left of her, had moved away.

'What is *wrong* with these dead people?' Delores growled under her breath.

Delores looked over her shoulder. Prudence was

sat bolt upright on her bed, pale and nervy, gripping her quilt so tightly that her knuckles threatened to burst through her skin. 'Please tell me she said something.'

Delores wished she could give Prudence the answer she wanted. 'I could hear her breathing, then singing some old rhyme about hide and seek, but when I tried to talk to her, she moved away, like…' Delores could hardly believe what she was about to say, '…like she didn't know I was there.'

Prudence's eyes were fixed on the door. 'And that's not a normal necromancy type situation?'

'No, it is not a normal necromancy type situation.' Delores reached for the dolls. They were lying face down on the step where she'd left them. The faded fabric of their clothes quivered as she turned them over, but their eyes were just painted marks, their lips pressed together in cherry bows. 'Come on, Agnes,' she said, trying to disguise the desperation in her voice, 'speak to me.' But Agnes and the dolls were no more present in this world than the bird whose skull sat on Delores' bedside table.

Delores put her eye up to the keyhole and waited for a flicker of movement. Then she slumped down with her back against the clocktower door. First the Tolbooth Bòcan had been unaware of her, though that wasn't so weird, but then there was the dead girl at Holyrood that looked straight past her, the fleeting shadows that made no attempt to catch her attention, and now Agnes.

'Do we ever lose our powers?' she asked Prudence.

'I hope this is a general question,' said Prudence, 'otherwise we're in big trouble.'

Delores adjusted the little stitched hat that the smaller doll was wearing and then put them back down on the step, holding her hand over them for a moment, hoping to feel something, a vague prickling of her skin, an uncanny cold spot.

'We're in big trouble,' she said, 'and we need to get out of here before Magoria calls the Gathering.'

18

The battle with Cook had taken its toll on Magoria. When Delores and Prudence snuck past her room, they could hear high-pitched snoring coming from her tiny nose as she dozed under the monstrous animal pelts. Her boots were lined up neatly by her bed and her beetle-like coat was hanging from the bed post, its sleeve pinned ready for repair. The sealskin bag was next to her boots and its fastening was open. The treacherous ledger that had sunk Oddvar was just visible. Delores nodded towards it and whispered, 'We could take it. She'd have less proof.'

'It wouldn't be the answer,' Prudence whispered. 'She's got too much on us.'

'Then we've nothing to lose.'

Delores nudged one boot off with the toe of the other, and then the second boot. She hitched her roaming socks back into place, almost wobbling over as she tried to balance on one leg. Prudence grabbed her arm to stop her falling, then shook her head at her, but Delores pulled away and crept into the room. She held her breath as she tiptoed towards the bag, keeping an eye on Magoria, listening to the pattern of her little snores for signs she might wake up. She knelt next to the bag, moving the ledger to one side, trying to edge it out without disturbing the bag or its owner. Tucked behind it was Bartleby's chess piece. Delores tried to slide the ledger out, but it was snagged on an inner pocket. She tugged at it gently, but it wouldn't shift. The little chess piece knocked against it as she tried.

Magoria snorted and held her breath.

Delores froze. Keeping her eyes firmly on Magoria, she tried to loosen the book. Her fingers ran along the inner folds of the bag and reached the chess piece again. Magoria rolled over and her arm lolled over the edge of the bed, missing Delores' nose by an angel's whisper. Delores closed her hand around the chess piece, then crept out backwards, not daring to breathe. She'd have that one small victory at least. Prudence rolled her eyes as Delores grabbed her boots, then followed Prudence silently into the dining room.

The fire was still burning. Gabriel was curled up asleep at Oddvar's feet, his tarot cards stacked neatly beside him. Prudence knelt and whispered, 'We have to go.'

Gabriel looked at them both, bleary from being woken up. 'Go where?'

'To Doctor Reid's,' answered Delores. 'We need to buy ourselves some time, try and figure out how to stop Magoria.'

Gabriel put his head back down, gazing into the fire. 'I'm not coming. I can't leave Oddvar on his own with her.'

'You have to,' said Delores. She could feel her panic rising; it was a dreadful choice for all of them. 'She wouldn't dare do anything to Oddvar, and she thinks she has what she needs. Please, I'm begging you Gabriel, come with us.'

Gabriel sat up, wrapping his arms around his knees. 'She doesn't have anything on me, nothing that would include me in a Gathering anyway, and I can't tell her any more than she already knows.'

Delores crouched next to him and took his hand, 'Please, Gabriel. Magoria will be furious when she finds out we're gone. I can't stand the thought of her taking it out on you. She'll go digging again, I know she will, especially if she thinks she can find a way to add you to the Gathering.'

Gabriel placed his other hand over hers and smiled. 'We all know divination comes with issues, but imprisonment in the jails of the North isn't one of them.' He sat up, crossed his legs, and ruffled his hair. His glasses were folded next to him, but he didn't put them on. He split his deck of tarot cards, then shuffled them back together and tapped on top of the deck three times.

'We haven't got time for this, Gabriel,' whispered Prudence. 'Magoria could wake any minute.'

'She won't,' he said. 'She already sent the message. The Gathering's underway. She's resting up for her big moment. Take a card.' He spread the deck in front of Delores with one smooth swipe.

Prudence was itching with frustration, so rather than argue, Delores quickly took a card from the middle. When she turned it over, her mouth went dry. The card looked horrific. It showed a tower with a man falling and a giant crown toppling from its battlements in a storm. She wouldn't forget it in a hurry.

'It's not as bad as it looks,' said Gabriel, 'and sometimes a card only makes sense later. This one?' He tapped the card. 'It's the Tower: a rebel card. Thinking of tearing down any hierarchies, Mackenzie? A government or two?'

Delores shook her head. 'Bit busy for that.'

Gabriel smiled and pressed his finger into the back of her hand, searching her near future for clues. 'I can see one of the dead close behind you,' he said, 'like literally on your heels.' Delores tried to pull away. He was seeing the only Bòcan currently aware of her existence and she didn't want that in her future whether Gabriel predicted it or not, but he refused to let go. 'And a woman,' he said, 'maybe your mother but she's hazy, and then another, your sister, I think, wearing … no that can't be right either.'

'Well?' said Prudence. 'Don't leave us in suspense.'

Gabriel shrugged. 'It's so stupid,' he said, 'but the clearest image was Sweet Shop Esme holding a grey monkey.'

'A monkey?' said Delores and Prudence in unison. They glared at each other. That was happening way too often.

Gabriel nodded. 'A *grey* monkey. No idea what species, which is annoyingly unspecific, so I don't know if it's a symbol, like of a circus or something.' He closed his eyes, grasping for more detail. 'Sorry,' he said, 'just basic monkey vibes. Sometimes it's as vague as the cards, especially if I'm tired.'

'Please come with us,' begged Delores.

Gabriel silently gathered his tarot cards together, straightening them by running his finger up the edge of the stack. He placed them to one side, and rested his head back against Oddvar's knees, smiling at noises coming from the kitchen: a pan being gently placed in the sink, the metallic sound of the cooking-range door clicking shut.

'Cook's awake,' said Gabriel. 'How could anything possibly go wrong?' He chuckled to himself but stopped abruptly when Prudence grabbed his arm and dragged him to his feet.

'Then let Cook keep an eye on Oddvar,' she said. 'You're coming with us.'

19

At the front of the Book Store, Delores folded Bartleby's blue blanket into a neat square and turned his basket the right way up. Prudence sighed at her, keeping a firm grip on Gabriel's arm.

'It's for when we get him back,' said Delores. 'He'll want to go to bed.' She stroked the top of the blanket, whispering, 'We will get you back.'

Prudence was struggling with the door. 'Magoria's locked it,' she snarled. She fumbled in her pocket for the almost-everything key.

'I'm not gonna do a runner,' said Gabriel, pulling his arm out of Prudence's grasp. 'It'd be a lot easier to open the door if you let go of me. And I need my coat.' Prudence managed to hang on to his shirt sleeve, but he yanked it out of her fingers. 'It's all right for you two in your…' he said, gesturing at them as if unsure what to call Prudence's new ensemble.

Prudence glared at him. 'Don't you dare try anything, Gabriel, or I swear...'

'As if... And it's just under the counter.' Gabriel put his arms up in surrender.

Prudence seemed to be making a mental estimate of the distance between the door and Gabriel's coat. She looked at Delores, waiting for back-up.

'Let him get his coat,' said Delores. 'You're being ridiculous.'

After a few miniscule adjustments of the key in the lock, Prudence got the door open. She adjusted her scarf and stepped out onto the street.

Delores heard a rushing of footsteps behind her. Two hands shoved her so hard between the shoulder blades that she fell forward, tripping on the door frame and crashing straight into Prudence. They both landed in an undignified heap in the middle of the pavement as the door slammed shut behind them. The almost-everything key went tumbling past Delores. She quickly grabbed it as it skidded towards the gutter. Prudence leapt up and banged her hands on the door. She yanked the handle and tried to force her way back in using her shoulder, managing to get it open a few centimetres before it was pushed back against her. Prudence briefly lost her balance, but it was long enough. There was a screech of wood against stone as Gabriel moved something up against it on the other side.

'You get out here right now, Gabriel Galbraith!' hissed Prudence through the keyhole. 'Do not make me compel you. You know I can.'

Delores righted herself and slipped the key into her inner pocket between the chess piece and the silver ball. She leaned over Prudence, mouth almost against the door. 'Come on, Gabriel,' she said. 'Please, *please* come with us.'

There was a moment's silence, and then Gabriel's voice came back through the keyhole. 'I'm staying with Oddvar. And if you try anything, Prudence, if I feel you anywhere inside my mind, *anywhere,* I swear I will scream until Magoria wakes up. Let's see you put your plan into action then.'

'You wouldn't,' whispered Prudence.

'Try me. I'll keep her busy, but it won't be long before she realises that you're gone. You told me too much already. You told me where you were going.'

Prudence sagged, banging her head in a gentle rhythm against the door. 'Then that's why you *have* come with us, Gabriel. Uncle Oddvar can protect himself. You're safer out here with us.'

Delores put her hand on Prudence's shoulder. 'I don't think it's just about Oddvar.'

Prudence turned her head from the door. 'What do you mean?'

'I think he's scared to leave the Tolbooth. He knows where everything is inside, how to get around. His eyesight's worse than he's letting on. Sweet Shop Esme said she hadn't seen him outside all summer. He hasn't even been to buy sherbet straws and you know how much he loves Bartleby.'

Prudence stood and dusted herself down. 'You're being ridiculous.'

'Am I? When was the last time *you* saw him go outside.'

Prudence thought for a moment, then slammed her hand against the door one last time. A light went on in one of the upper rooms.

Delores gently took hold of Prudence's arm. 'We have to go.'

Prudence groaned as they turned away. Sweet Shop Esme was flapping her arms at them from the other side of the road. Prudence put her head down and was about to march off when Delores stopped her.

'Doctor Reid said we should trust Esme, and hasn't she always been kind to us?'

'Kind? You think we have time for *kind?* And she's a Normal, through and through, about as much use as a…' Prudence stopped halfway towards the insult that was casually brewing in her mind. 'Grey monkey,' she whispered.

'That,' said Delores, 'is the least sense you've made all day and let's face it…'

Prudence marched across the street before Delores could finish speaking.

Esme flinched and took a step back as Prudence stormed towards her. She bent to the side of Prudence with a pleading look accompanied by a more subtle but desperate wave at Delores. Whatever was going on, Esme was most definitely not holding a grey monkey. A grey monkey would have slowed her down as she ran inside the shop.

Delores and Prudence bundled in through the door, though Delores still had no idea why.

Esme was searching behind the counter for something as Prudence placed her hands on the glass cabinet and leaned over to see what was going on.

'Well?' said Prudence. 'What do you want? We're kind of in a hurry.'

'Yes, yes,' said Esme. 'On your way to Ernaline's no doubt. I've seen her in and out of the Tolbooth all summer. And that scrappy-looking woman in the magician's coat.'

Delores snorted a laugh. 'Oh, you mean Magoria? She's not a magician, she's…'

Delores heard Prudence's voice inside her head telling her to shut up. She obliged, suddenly aware of how they must look to Normals, how Normals matched what they saw to what they thought believable.

'I knew it was here somewhere,' said Esme. She popped up from behind the counter waving a plain white paper bag in her hand.

When Prudence screwed her face up at her in confusion, Esme added, 'Sorry, it was all I had to hand when those awful, *awful* men came and took your little grey monkey away.'

'Our … little grey monkey?' asked Delores, hardly daring to hope.

Prudence reached out for the bag, but Esme gave her the side-eye and handed it to Delores. 'Do you need to make it so obvious how you feel about me, Prudence?' said Esme. 'And yes, I do know your name. I know all your names.'

Prudence had the good grace to blush. 'I'm sorry,' she said. 'Could I start again? What do you mean *our little grey monkey?*'

Esme brightened, quicker to forgive Prudence's rudeness than she deserved. 'The one that holds the door open for you,' she said. 'I've seen you handing him the blue sherbet straws you buy. Are they really that good for him by the way? I didn't know monkeys ate sherbet. Funny little thing though, isn't he? Even for a monkey.'

Delores thought carefully about her next question. 'You can see him … moving?'

Esme nodded. 'Of course! He's almost as rude as…' She paused as her eyes flickered towards Prudence. 'Let's just say he's not super friendly. He lets the door go in my face every time I try to come in for a book. Shame. Would love to get a proper look at him but he's always back in his basket, still as stone under that cute little blanket.' Esme glanced from Delores to Prudence, then back to Delores. Delores realised both of their mouths were gaping wider and wider as Esme spoke. Delores gave a quick cough to clear her throat and elbowed Prudence out of her stunned silence. Her hand shook as she unfolded the sweet bag, revealing a company name hastily scribbled on it.

Guillemot & Bombina
Architectural Salvage & Fine Art Exports

'That's the name on the side of the van they put him in,' said Esme. 'Though what a fine art exporter would want with a monkey, Heaven alone knows.

That magician woman just stood there too, watching. Funny thing though,' said Esme, 'tried to find *Guillemot & Bombina* online but nothing. I mean, what kind of company doesn't advertise online these days?' Esme glanced over Delores' shoulder towards the Tolbooth. She blushed. 'I didn't mean…'

'Don't worry,' said Delores. 'Is there any way we can find them?'

Esme smiled and leaned over the counter, lowering her voice to an excited whisper. 'I asked around,' she said. 'Other business owners, that kind of thing. Apparently, it's an odd little place under one of the arches along Cowgate, the one just past Whiskey Row. Never open. Goodness knows how they make any money, but maybe you can go get your monkey back.'

Delores daren't look at Prudence. Instead, she watched Esme as she reached for the jar of blue sherbet straws and slowly opened it. She took a handful of them and put them in a paper bag, tying it with the same black and white string that had been tied around Doctor Reid's bag of barley twists. Delores took the almost empty bag from her pocket.

'Oh,' said Esme, 'need a refill?' She placed the sherbet straws on the counter and took the bag from Delores. As Esme ran her hand across the barley-twist bag, the same look washed over her face as when Prudence, Doctor Reid and even Obsidian Strange looked at Gabriel's moth drawings. Delight. 'Doctor Reid's favourites,' she whispered. 'You are a funny lot.' She took a silver scoop and made up a fresh bag of barley twists, palming the original bag into the pocket of her cotton apron.

'We don't have any money,' said Delores.

'Don't worry,' said Esme. 'I'll put them on Doctor Reid's account. I'm sure she won't mind, and I know she's good for it. Always cash. Every Friday without fail. Here.' Esme finished off both bundles with a hand-stamped brown cardboard tag and handed them to Delores. 'One for you, one for the wee monkey.'

'He's called Bartleby,' said Delores.

Esme smiled. 'What a great name for a monkey! Hope you find him soon. Those men looked awful.'

Delores tucked the sweets into her outer pocket and handed the sherbet straws to Prudence as she stepped round her towards the space between the glass cases crammed with Halloween treats.

'What are you doing?' muttered Prudence.

Esme met Delores halfway, smiling. 'Off you go then,' she said.

Delores threw her arms around Esme's neck and pulled her in for a tight hug. Esme tensed at first but quickly softened, rubbing Delores' back. Delores breathed in the mixture of scented soap and sweet spun sugar. 'Thank you,' she whispered. 'Ernaline was right about you.'

Esme gently pulled away and chucked Delores under her chin. 'My pleasure. Now go get your wee monkey back. And if you fancy the Fire Festival later…?'

Delores looked at the poster again, the looming tower. She shuddered. 'Thanks, but we have stuff to do, and finding Bartleby is just the start, right Prudence?'

Prudence nodded, tight lipped for a moment, as if weighing up their options. 'Agreed,' she said. 'Bartleby first. Let's hope they haven't shipped him off to Paris yet. We can hide him at Doctor Reid's.'

'Hide him?' said Esme. 'Why would you need to…?'

Delores was about to come up with a perfectly plausible reason when Prudence grabbed her by the coat sleeve and dragged her out of the door.

20

By the time Delores and Prudence reached the archway, the afternoon light was fading. Parked on the pavement next to a door that towered above them, was a van, part covered in tarpaulin and sporting a bright yellow wheel clamp. A group of Australians singing loudly outside a bar on the opposite side of the street drew the attention of passers-by away from Prudence as she lifted the tarpaulin, revealing the first few letters painted on the van's side,

Guillem…

Architectural Sal……………

'It's them,' she shouted over the noise of the merrymakers.

Delores tried the doors at the back of the van, but they were locked. 'Not like he'd still be in there, anyway,' she said. 'Way too easy. Ideas?'

'If they transport valuable things,' said Prudence,

'the van might have an alarm.' Prudence gestured towards a narrow cutting at the side of the archway. It was ankle deep in rubbish and as Delores got closer, it was obvious it was regularly used by the neighbourhood cats as a toilet. At least she hoped it was cats.

'How about actually *trying* to get out of sight?' said Prudence, flapping her hands at Delores to move further back.

Delores slithered barely a body width into the opening. She held her breath and prayed it was litter she was stepping in. Prudence placed her palms against the side of the van, checking either way for people coming along the pavement. She leaned into it hard and shoved it until it started to rock. The singers at the bar opposite spotted what she was doing and gave a loud cheer. To Delores' horror, Prudence was quickly joined by two men from the crowd and together they rocked the van so hard that the alarm was triggered. A screeching siren blasted up into the arches, bouncing helter-skelter off every piece of brick and metal it was made of. Prudence squeezed in next to Delores in the hiding spot as the two men ran back laughing to join their friends.

In less than a minute, the door under the archway was pulled open. A man lumbered out, the shorter of the two they'd seen outside the bookstore, the men that took Bartleby away.

'Bombina,' whispered Prudence as the man fumbled with his keys. When he noticed the wheel clamp, he kicked it hard then jumped about holding his foot, but all that could be heard was the van's alarm and the shrieking of the crowd opposite. Bombina screamed and yelled at them, shaking his fists and spitting only to be met with more jeers and applause as he dropped his keys. When he bent down to find them, Prudence grabbed Delores' sleeve and they slipped inside, spotted only by the raucous group who cheered and clapped even harder.

Prudence pulled Delores behind the open door into an enclosed courtyard, bumping straight into the statue of a weeping angel. They scurried into the shadows behind it as the alarm stopped. After more swearing and the rustling of tarpaulin, the man came back inside. He used both hands and his full body weight to push the door closed again and drag a bolt across it.

As the bolt clicked into place, Delores got the familiar creeping sensation that warned her something else was in the dark with them; the faint smell of camphor confirmed that the something was not good.

Bombina marched back across the courtyard. Delores and Prudence heard another door open, and a low light lit up the enormity of space they were hiding in. It had a high, vaulted, brick ceiling, and they could hear traffic rumbling across the bridge far above them. The air was stale and thick with falling dust, and broken gravestones lay scattered across the floor. In front of them was a small, self-contained building that looked as if it had been transported brick by brick to the courtyard and then reassembled by someone who'd never seen the original plan. It had one oddly unsymmetrical window, and the battered door was slightly ajar. Bombina stopped abruptly, one foot on the doorstep. He checked over his shoulder, gazing into the shadows. Delores and Prudence pushed further back into the dark, holding their breath until finally Bombina shrugged and went inside.

Prudence picked her way through the discarded gravestones. Delores followed, constantly alert. The stones might not mark burial spots now, but they did once. Some were elaborately carved with skulls wearing wreaths of flowers, others were flatter and plain with simple crosses and long-forgotten names that hadn't been spoken in centuries. It was the kind of place Delores would instinctively avoid, afraid of being overwhelmed by the reluctant dead. The hairs on her neck were still prickling but all she could see were fleeting shadows. She turned her head to the side, trying to make them sharper in the corner of her eye, to separate them into individuals, but as the shadows stalked the edges of the courtyard, not one of them approached her. She breathed a sigh of relief and stepped forward to catch up with Prudence.

Until.

A singular feeling. Crisp. Sharp. Cold.

Something was close behind her, running a nail down her neck, leaning in, a whisper of breath in her ear, a gut-wrenchingly familiar smell. Delores drew her hand slowly to the back of her neck, feeling the nobble of the bone at the top of her spine. She expected to feel a ghostly hand meet hers, the touch of a Bòcan, but instead it was a gentle ripple of laughter that brushed against her fingers, and a deep voice whispered, 'Welcome to the house of Hartigan Fox.'

There was a rush of air as the Bòcan stepped away and when Delores turned, she saw a scattering of dried flower petals drifting to the floor. She reached out and caught the last ones on her outstretched palm as a deeper swirling of blackness disappeared behind the weeping angel.

'Don't just stand there gawping,' whispered Prudence from the door of the strange little house.

She ushered Delores forward, but Delores' head was swimming. If she took one more step, she knew she would fall. Her hands shook as she took the bag of sweets from her pocket. Her fingers were trembling too much to undo the string. The bag ripped and half of the sweets scattered across the floor. Prudence looked furious as the sweets skidded over the stones. Delores quickly closed her hand around the few that were left. She put one of the barley twists in her mouth and stashed the rest loose in her pocket. A dark chasm was growing in her chest, something was becoming absent, lost, trickling away to form a bigger hole, and it was making her dizzy and anxious. The Bòcan was getting stronger, more cunning and she was starting to suspect it was stealing more than her energy.

The anxiety subsided as the sugar surged into Delores' system. Esme's sweets packed a bigger punch than they ought to; it was a mystery how she did it. Maybe Esme wasn't as Normal as she seemed. She took a deep breath to steady herself and staggered forward, sinking down against the wall next to Prudence.

'What is wrong with you?' hissed Prudence.

'He was just here,' said Delores. 'Hartigan Fox.' She held out the petals in her hand.

Prudence screwed her eyes up, struggling to see the tiny petals in the dark. She held them up to the light from the window, then let them fall through her fingers to the ground. She looked over Delores' shoulder, into the dark behind them. 'Like we don't have enough to worry about. Has he gone?'

'For now,' said Delores. She got to her knees so that she could see in through the grimy window. Inside, the room was stuffed with old fireplaces, giant mirrors and extravagant gilded picture frames. A model of a trapeze artist dressed in a red and gold corset swooped down, suspended from the ceiling in an acrobatic pose. There was a statue wrapped in robes wearing a traffic cone on its head and old carnival boards were propped up against a wall, their orange and red lettering advertising helter-skelter rides and penny-a-go games. There was no sign of Bartleby.

In the centre of the room a small electric fire glowed three bright bars of heat against Guillemot and Bombina's ankles. They were playing cards on a rickety table surrounded by empty cans and takeaway wrappers. Bombina took off his jacket and tugged at his collar. As he leaned to take another card, a heavy silver object on a long chain swung forward and hit the table. Delores pressed her nose harder up against the grime of the window, trying to see what it was, but Bombina was too far away. She scoped what she could of the room again, hoping to find any clue that

Bartleby was still there, and not in some shipping crate on his way back to his old master in Paris.

She flopped back down next to Prudence. 'Nothing. What do we do now?'

'We ring the bell,' said Prudence.

'We *what?*'

Delores grabbed at Prudence's coat as she stood, trying to pull her back down, but it was too late. The bell had been rung and Prudence smoothed the front of her coat, readying herself to cast whatever illusion it would take to get their beloved Bartleby back.

21

The door was flung open, and a red-faced Bombina stood glaring at Delores and Prudence. Without the woolly hat he'd been wearing at the Tolbooth, they could see he was almost bald, and the few hairs he did have had been smoothed down with a clear, oily goop. His white shirt sleeves were rolled up above his elbows and the black waistcoat that covered it was grubby and over-tight. As he gripped the edge of the door, his fingers glinted in the light. They were crammed with chunky lumps of gold set with coins and bulbous silver rings. His thumb was covered base to knuckle by a deep red enamel heart topped with a golden crown. As he leaned out to get a better look at his visitors, a heavy skull-shaped pendant swung to one side. He caught Delores staring and tucked it inside his waistcoat.

'You're trespassin',' he growled. 'We don't allow trespassin', do we, Guillemot?'

There was a shuffling sound as Guillemot lurched into view, his shiny black hair streaked through on the top with a thick slice of white. He was dressed the same as Bombina, down to the exact folds in his sleeves, but his fingers were bare and agile as he played with a piece of red string. He twisted the thread into intricate shapes, not once pausing to look at his handiwork. Delores and Prudence stood in silence, waiting for his reply. They could hear a clock ticking somewhere deep inside the strange little house and when it chimed, Guillemot startled and said, 'No, we do *not* allow trespassin', Bombina.' His beady black eyes fixed on Delores and Prudence. 'Shall I fetch the beating stick?'

Prudence quickly said, 'No need for a beating stick. We're not trespassers. We're here to do business.'

Both men nodded in unison. Guillemot played with his string, while Bombina gripped the door a little tighter, surveying Prudence's outfit from her boots to her collar.

His stare lingered just a little too long on her scarf and she reached up to feel along its edge, checking discreetly for feathers.

'Don't I know you?' asked Bombina, slyly.

Delores and Prudence shook their heads. 'I doubt it,' said Prudence. 'We're traders. New to the city.'

'Bit young for traders,' said Bombina. He narrowed his eyes and made gurgling noises deep in his throat as he pondered. Finally, he spoke. 'You can leave the way you came. We do not do business with children, do we, Guillemot?'

'We do not,' confirmed Guillemot. He kept nodding as he formed the outline of a pyramid with his string, his index fingers pointing skyward.

Bombina tried to close the door, but Prudence stuck her boot inside, yelping as the door crushed against it. Bombina tutted and gave it another quick shove. Prudence pulled her foot out and the door slammed shut.

'What are you waiting for?' asked Delores. 'Do your thing. Tell them to let us in.'

'Don't you think I tried? The two of them are connected somehow, twisting in and out of each other's ideas. You've heard how they speak? It's the same with their brains. Bombina's the boss but Guillemot's bumbling in and out of his thoughts. There's no space left for me to work. I'll figure it out, but meanwhile, follow my lead.' She bent down and called through the letter box. 'But we have something for you. A rare collector's piece.'

There was muttering and shuffling behind the door. A minute later, it creaked open again. Prudence nodded towards the rings on Bombina's fingers. 'I can see you're a man of … taste and this is a once in a lifetime opportunity.' She turned to Delores, smiling in a way that didn't fit her face. 'Give me the thing.'

Delores stared back at her, unblinking. She reached into her inside pocket and ran her hand over the silver ball. She heard Prudence clearly in her head, *Not* that *thing! The chess piece.*

'How did you…?' Delores stopped mid-sentence. Of course, Prudence knew she'd taken it. She shook her head, but worse than Prudence's angry glare was the sudden interest shown by Guillemot and Bombina. Guillemot stopped playing his game and Bombina let go of the door. He hopped onto the step, toppling an empty milk bottle that spun away across the ground. 'Show me,' he said.

Delores wrapped her fingers around the little soldier. The carvings on its face pressed against her skin, reminding her how much Bartleby loved it. As she took it from her pocket, Bombina reached out, but Delores pulled away. Prudence stepped between them. 'Can we come in?' she asked. 'You need good light to see how special this piece is.'

Guillemot whispered in Bombina's ear, both

men keeping their eyes on Delores' hand. Bombina nodded and they both moved back, standing either side of the hall as Delores and Prudence passed between them.

The metal lamps screwed haphazardly to the peeling walls flickered and hissed in the cold, narrow hall. A dark wood staircase led up to a loft and two pairs of slippers sat neatly side by side on the first step.

'Has this always been your house?' asked Delores as she walked slowly along the hallway. She stopped when she noticed an old-fashioned black pram half tucked away in the space under the stairs. It had big white wheels with rusting metal spokes and a stiff hood that was pulled all the way up.

'Funny you should ask,' said Bombina, a glimmer of pride in his voice. 'It was a knock-down house. We traded goods for all its bits and parts. Rebuilt it here.'

'Rebuilt it,' echoed Guillemot. 'Clever trading that was, Bombina.'

'Interesting,' said Delores stepping closer to the pram. There was a cover made of the same material but instead of a space to peep in at a baby, thick wire mesh had been stapled between the hood and the cover. Inside the pram, something was snoring and when it grumbled in its sleep, Delores and Prudence looked at each other. There was a gnashing of stone teeth between snores.

Delores reached out for the pram, but Prudence stepped in front of her. 'Not yet.' She looked past Delores' shoulder as Bombina closed the door and turned the catch. He held one hand over a small combination lock, turning the dials in secret. Delores spun round as the lock clicked into place.

'You don't want to be out there amongst the gravestones when the dark things come,' said Bombina. 'Follow me, children.'

There were no echoes of agreement from Guillemot this time, just sinister chortling as he untangled his fingers from the red string and placed it carefully in his pocket.

22

Bombina dragged two small stools from under a pile of old newspapers and placed them at the card table. The room was even more cluttered than it had looked from the window, stuffed with carnival costumes and masks that hung from nails on the walls. Below these was a puppet theatre fronted by three tiny taxidermy monkeys dressed in threadbare britches and tailcoats. Their angry faces were framed by tufts of faded gold fur; one had a cello, one a violin and one a set of cymbals. Their glazed eyes seemed to follow Delores no matter where she moved. She stared back at them and as she stepped towards the table, she banged her shins on the head and shoulders of a wooden clown. As the clown rocked forward, a hard cork ball fell from its gawping mouth and rolled towards Bombina. Bombina trapped the ball under his boot. 'Sit down and keep both hands where I can see them.' He threw the ball back at the clown's mouth, making a vicious but perfect shot. The ball rattled the back of the clown's throat and clunked down inside him. Delores swore she heard the clown snarl as they took their places at the table.

Guillemot whispered in Bombina's ear. 'Ask them what they've got to trade.'

Delores placed the chess piece in the centre of the table, keeping hold of it. 'Like my colleague told you,' she said, trying her best to sound confident, 'it's a rare item.'

'Colleague now, is it?' said Bombina, grinning slyly. 'Doesn't look rare to me.'

Guillemot nodded. 'We only trade in rare.'

'Of course,' said Prudence, looking around the room stuffed with Guillemot and Bombina's *rarities*. 'This is a genuine piece, cunningly acquired from the Museum of Scotland. A Viking chess piece, but with, how shall I say…' She paused, cocking her head to one side.

'Just say,' grumbled Bombina. 'I am getting bored.'

'Powers,' said Prudence. 'This piece has powers in the carvings on the shield, powers that can haunt people with their deepest fears. You could sell it for an absolute fortune.' She turned to speak to Delores. 'You can let go of it. These men are honest traders. They probably have a licence and everything.'

'Licence,' nodded Guillemot, 'and a beating stick.' He reached behind him and grabbed a smooth, shiny piece of wood that had been concealed by one of the carnival boards. It was longer than a baseball bat and twice as brutal looking.

Delores kicked Prudence under the table. She heard Prudence's voice inside her head. *I told you. Follow my lead.*

Delores let go of the chess piece and Prudence slid it towards Bombina, keeping one finger on its head. Bombina reached inside his waistcoat and pulled out a magnifying glass, dislodging the skull pendant that he'd hidden earlier. The pendant knocked against the table as he leaned in to take a closer look at what Prudence was offering. Delores stared hard at the silver skull, taking in every detail. She was sure it was the same one Hartigan Fox was holding up to the camera in the newspaper clipping. The Bòcain always had that one thing that connected them to the living world, something that still existed as a real object, a thing they loved but that also made it possible to defeat them. Delores had to have that pendant.

'What do they want for it?' Guillemot asked Bombina, drawing Delores' attention back to the task in hand.

Bombina's eyes flickered between Delores and

Prudence. 'I know what it is they want, Guillemot. They want the little demon we have in the hallway. Saw the skinny black-haired one eying it up. They think we're stupid, Guillemot, but we are not.'

'No,' said Guillemot. 'We are not stupid. And the demon is mine. Aye, clever little demon, that he is.'

'That he is,' repeated Bombina. 'But so are we and not to be high jinxed by children. Children that might go telling tales of demons kept in Edinburgh that should've straight away been sent onwards to their Paris master.'

'You're wrong,' said Delores. 'We really are traders. Started young. Isn't that right, Prudence?' She gave Prudence another quick kick under the table and got a sharp one back. 'We don't know about any demon, and even if we did who would we tell?'

There was a quick flash of *what in all-Heavens are you doing?* in her mind from Prudence but Delores pushed the thought away. She could feel threat hanging heavy in the air and they weren't escaping without a fight. She'd have little to no chance of wrestling the pendant from Bombina in a scuffle. They'd make a grab for Bartleby on the way out. No man left behind.

Delores cleared her throat. 'While your demon story is super-interesting, Mr Bombina, what we really want is that skull pendant.'

Prudence chimed in with, 'The chess piece for the skull *and* the demon. My associate doesn't know what she's talking about. The chess piece is more valuable than both of those items put together.'

Bombina laughed as he ran his hands over the silver skull. 'This is not for children. It gets heavy when the dark turns thicker, and things grow cold.' He shuddered at the thought and then leaned across the table, lowering his voice, 'Too heavy for scrawny necks. Necks that easily…'

'Snap!' shouted Guillemot.

'I'm not scared of the dark or the chills,' said Delores. 'But you seem to be, so why not trade it?'

Bombina narrowed his eyes. 'I'll tell you why not. I know it was you outside the Tolbooth when we came to collect the little demon. If this is Prudence, then *you* are Delores and I know exactly who you'd tell. Then we'd be for the prisons of the North, just like you.'

Delores shook her head frantically. 'We wouldn't, I swear!'

'We wouldn't,' added Prudence. 'You've got us all wrong, Mr Bombina.'

Bombina slammed his hand on the table. 'The demon shouted for you, he did, *Don't let them send me back, boo hoo*!' Bombina bundled his fists and rubbed at his eyes, mimicking Bartleby. 'And then that boy comes runnin',' Bombina was laughing now, so hard that he could hardly get the words out, 'but we dragged him upstairs, didn't we, Guillemot?'

Guillemot nodded and reached back into his pocket for his red thread. He put his fingers back through the strands, winding new shapes. 'We didn't have the beating stick, but we roughed him around anyway, didn't we, Bombina?'

Bombina nodded, tears of laughter streaming from his eyes. 'Good times, Guillemot, good times. Cried just like the little demon, didn't he?' Guillemot didn't answer; he was too busy choking on his own snickety giggles as he played with his red string.

Delores felt Prudence bristle with anger beside her, struggling to keep control, but when she saw the tip of Prudence's tongue poking out between her teeth, Delores knew she'd found a way in. Maybe it was their sudden good mood that had opened them up, or the fun they were having thinking about the horrible things they'd done. Whatever it was, Bombina and Guillemot were about to experience one apocalyptic-grade illusion. They didn't have a clue what was about to hit them, but Delores was sure they deserved every high-definition, mind-blowing moment of it.

Delores looked around her at the untethered

objects in the room. She'd seen what happened when Prudence lost it. *Telekinesis under duress* Magoria had called it; the ability to move objects when she was angry. Delores had only seen Prudence throwing knives once but that had been enough to scare both the living and the dead. That level of scare would be pretty useful right now, and so would a place to take cover.

Delores slid to the floor holding on to the table leg. She peeped up over the table's edge as the little soldier chess piece and the playing cards started to vibrate. Puzzled, Bombina placed his hands flat on the tabletop. He pressed it down to steady the moving objects whilst trying to figure out why Delores was on the floor.

Prudence switched her gaze to Guillemot. His fingers went faster and faster amongst his red thread, twisting and turning it, making ever more complex shapes until the thread knotted itself tight around his fingers. He looked around him, at Prudence, at Bombina, then back to his hands, hands he no longer had control over. He tried to pull them apart, but the threads pulled tighter until he screamed with frustration. Bombina leaned across the table, snatching at Prudence's lapels. 'Stop it!' he shrieked. 'Wicked child!' He shook her hard. Prudence sagged a little in his grip, biting gently on her tongue and smiling at Bombina. He let go.

Bombina flopped back in his chair and watched in horror. The hanging trapeze artist swayed back and forth on her ropes to music played by the band of mechanical monkeys, the tempo of the screeching violin and demonic cello marked by the clashing of the middle monkey's cymbals. The carnival boards rattled against the walls as the music reached fever-pitch, then fell to the floor. The mice that had been living behind them scattered across the room. As Delores watched them run, she struggled to know what was real or if she was being dragged into the edge of Prudence's illusion, and it was terrifying.

The wooden clown creaked and groaned, rattling its base against the floor. A low rumbling noise came from its throat and Delores ducked her head under the table as a hard cork ball flew from its mouth, hurtling towards Guillemot. He leaped from his chair, dodging the first, but it was quickly followed by a barrage that struck him about the shoulders and legs until he fell screaming to the floor, holding his tangled hands above his head for protection.

Delores was almost feeling sorry for them when she heard Prudence's voice shouting inside her head. *Get Bartleby, I can't do this much longer.*

Delores snatched up the little soldier and leaned across the table to a petrified Bombina. She cautiously lifted the chain and its skull pendant from around his indignant neck. She expected him to grab her at any moment, but he was too busy gripping the chair, transfixed by the chaos around him. The pendant was heavy, but Delores was sure it was not just the weight that made her arm ache as she slipped it round her neck. Something didn't want her to have it and she was sure that something was Hartigan Fox.

Delores kept herself low enough to avoid the flying debris as she ran to get Bartleby. He was wide awake as she skidded into the hallway, yanking furiously at the metal grid and chewing at its edges. 'Mon Dieu!' he shouted above the cacophony. 'What is happening?'

Delores tried pulling at the metal grid from her side, but it wouldn't shift. 'This, Bartleby L'Aubespine, is a rescue!'

When she was sure the grid wouldn't break, Delores pulled the pram from under the stairs and ran with it to the front door. She screamed, 'Prudence!' and there was a thudding crash as the flying objects fell the floor.

Prudence stepped quietly into the hallway. Her expression was calm, but her hands hung trembling by her sides and her skin was ashen. When Delores looked past her, Bombina was slouched in his chair, his face frozen in horror. Guillemot was kneeling next to him, his bound hands still protecting his head as he wept.

'That was some scary old do-dah you pulled there,' said Delores. 'Are you OK?'

'No, not really. I've never been that angry before,' said Prudence. Her voice barely reached above the silence as she adjusted her cuffs and checked her scarf. 'I don't know how long they'll stay like that. We should go.'

Delores rattled the door handle. 'All-Hell,' she groaned. 'The creep locked it. Any guesses at the combination?'

'Le jour de Noël,' grumbled Bartleby. 'Christmas day is the birthday of Monsieur Bombina.'

Delores slid the dials of the combination into place, *2.5.1.2.* The lock clicked open. 'Nice one, Bartleby,' she said. 'Great to have you back on the team.'

Delores and Prudence ran across the courtyard. They pushed and pulled the pram in and out of the gravestones and monuments while Bartleby muttered and grumbled about revenge and blue sherbet, biting at the metal grid that still held him prisoner.

Prudence used what strength she had left to swing the door open. She stepped back into Cowgate to more cheers from the party people outside the bar on the other side of the street.

Delores bumped the pram over the step and was just about to cross the threshold when she felt the cold hard drag on the back of her neck, and that pungent smell. She felt a hand run down her arm and it gripped her wrist as she reached for the skull pendant. Her instinct was right. She'd stumbled across the singular object she could use to destroy Hartigan Fox.

Prudence turned to look at her, wrought with frustration.

Bartleby stopped rattling at the metal and peered past Delores' shoulder. 'Mort-vivant,' he whispered. 'The un-dead is with us.'

Delores tried to pull free, but the chasm in her chest was growing deeper. She could feel herself being spun round. She needed that pocket of energy held in the pit of her stomach, the energy she should drag up through her chest until she could push Hartigan Fox away but the harder she tried, the stronger his grip, as if he was using her own power against her. In the dim light she could see his face, leering and eager. His mask was still in place over his ice-blue eyes and tendrils of red hair spilled over the top of it as he reached for Delores' neck. She pulled back, trying to summon the words she needed. Her lips were moving but no sound was coming out. Hartigan turned his head and put his ear to her mouth. The sallow skin that bunched slightly against the lower edge of his mask thinned and pulled tight against his cheekbones as he grinned at what she was trying to say.

Delores sucked in the dank air that surrounded them and focused on the few simple words that should drive him back. 'This is my domain,' she gasped. 'And you are uninvited.' She directed one last push of energy at the hand that gripped her. She squeezed her eyes closed, gritted her teeth and snarled through them with effort. She felt the slightest of slips and Hartigan's grip loosened enough for Delores to yank her hand free. She spun round towards the door and screamed, 'Run!'

Prudence did not wait for an explanation.

23

Delores pushed the pram along the streets that would lead them back up the hill, across the Royal Mile and into the safety of Doctor Reid's apartment in Ladystairs Close. Bartleby hung on to the metal grill as the pram's wonky wheels made it lurch and skitter on the uneven roads and pavements, while Prudence cleared the way ahead.

As they hurtled through the archway, Doctor Reid opened the door to the museum and ushered them inside. She nodded quickly at Prudence, saying that the image that had flashed into her mind of Bartleby's rescue was so startling that she'd dropped a valuable bottle of fever essence. Delores could not deny that Prudence S-Dottir's psychic gifts were a trump card.

Findo was waiting inside the door with some pliers and worked quickly to cut a hole big enough to drag Bartleby through. Delores tried to lift him, but her arms were shaking, and she could barely summon the strength to breathe, let alone lift a demon made of stone. Whilst Prudence whispered quickly to Doctor Reid, Findo lifted Bartleby into his arms and ushered Delores up the step ladder. She sighed with relief when she saw the blue troll cross was still on the underside of the door. They'd be safe from Hartigan Fox while she had time to figure it all out.

Bartleby climbed the last step himself and crawled over to the little black stove, whilst Findo disappeared back down the stepladder. Elijah was in his usual seat and slid further under his blanket at the sight of the strange, bad-tempered creature that was making himself at home on the hearth. As Bartleby warmed his clawed fingers and grumbled to himself, Elijah slipped carefully from his spot and placed his hand on Bartleby's shoulder. Before Delores could warn him about Bartleby's grumpiness and sharp teeth, the little demon relaxed. Elijah closed his eyes and brought his breathing in time with Bartleby's. Bartleby reached back and patted the boy's hand. Elijah nodded, smiled and then draped his blanket over Bartleby's shoulders. Bartleby sighed away a deep breath and within moments was sound asleep.

Noticing Delores and Prudence standing with

their mouths open, Elijah shrugged and said, 'I like him, so I made him feel better.'

As Elijah slid back into his cosy chair, Prudence asked, 'And what if you don't like somebody?'

Elijah's cheeks flushed but he held Prudence's gaze until she looked away, paler than ever.

This time, Doctor Reid was prepared for their visit. She leaned gently against the bookcase and slipped into the kitchen space behind, returning with a tray full of cakes and sandwiches from Tilly Whitlock's bakery. Delores' eyes roamed the feast, searching for the cherry fondant biscuits she been so tempted by only yesterday. That trip to Cormican's seemed a lifetime ago. As she sank her teeth into the soft white icing, she breathed a sigh of relief. Prudence chose a cupcake topped with a swirl of buttercream and tiny silver baubles that cracked like popcorn between her teeth. To Prudence's annoyance, Elijah chose the same. She scowled at him with every dainty nibble she took.

Delores nudged Prudence's foot with hers. 'It wasn't his fault.'

'Indeed,' said Doctor Reid, swooping in to join them.

Delores felt calmer as Doctor Reid's powdery scent filled the air and everything seemed brighter, even Bombina and Guillemot seemed ridiculous. When Doctor Reid caught Delores' eye, she moved away slightly and the feeling moved away with her, letting a much darker reality rush back in.

'I'm afraid I have some troubling news,' said Doctor Reid. 'The historian I told you about confirmed the stories about Hartigan Fox. He lived in Edinburgh in the 1980s, unhappy, belittled by his contemporaries for his single Gift; he could make any plant grow, no matter how rare.'

'But that's an amazing Gift,' said Elijah, 'better than dead things speaking to you.'

'Agreed,' said Delores.

'Anything has to be better than that,' added Prudence, biting into her cake.

'We can debate that later,' said Doctor Reid, trying to stay on track. 'He took a small cottage on the edge of the Botanic Gardens and studied plants and potions, growing ever more resentful of others' Gifts. Then he came across the makings of a potion that made their Gifts *available* to him.'

Delores placed her half-eaten biscuit back on the edge of the tray. 'He was collecting extra Gifts?'

'Yes, exactly,' replied Doctor Reid.

'But that shouldn't be possible,' said Prudence. 'Our Gifts are part of us.'

'He found a way,' said Doctor Reid. 'Extract of hound's tooth orchid, a strange plant only Hartigan could grow. That's the extra ingredient in his petals. Goodness knows what darkness overcame him, locked away in that cottage with his experiments.'

Delores already knew the answer to her next question, but she had to be certain. 'What happened to the cottage?'

'Demolished after his death,' said Doctor Reid. 'Every piece removed by an Old Town salvage company.'

'Guillemot and Bombina,' said Prudence. 'Those creeps rebuilt it, didn't they? They're living in it!'

'One of two reasons Hartigan Fox was hanging out there,' said Delores. She reached for the skull pendant. It felt so heavy that she could hardly lift it to show everyone. 'They must have *salvaged* this as well. What happened to the Paranormals he stole from?'

Doctor Reid shifted on the arm of the chair she was perched on. 'They died soon after, drained of even the power to take a sip of water, a breath of air. In effect, Hartigan Fox was a murderer. The night of the Halloween Ball...'

'What ball?' asked Prudence, shaking her head. 'If there was a society ball, I'd know.'

'Sure,' sighed Delores, trying to process everything

she was hearing, ''cos if there was a ball, you'd totally be queen of it.'

Elijah snorted a laugh, but Prudence didn't glare at him this time. She leaned forward in her seat, easing the pressure of the chair back on her shoulder blades, then reached inside her coat for the last of her ambergris. After swallowing, she gave a deep sigh and handed the bottle to Doctor Reid's outstretched hand.

'The ball was disbanded,' continued Doctor Reid, 'the year Hartigan Fox was discovered trying to poison another Paranormal with his concoctions. She too was a necromancer, Delores, a power he had yet to add to his collection.'

Delores and Doctor Reid exchanged worried glances.

A short but intense silence was broken by the cracking of the wood inside the fiery stove and the snapping of Prudence's patience. 'Anyone going to fill me in before I go looking for answers?'

'That's what all of this has been about,' said Delores. She held up the skull pendant and watched as it turned in the light. 'My necromancy. I thought I was controlling it when we first got back to the city but then it felt like it was drifting away, bit by bit. So *stupid* not to link that to Hartigan and his petals. That creeper's been stealing my Gift.'

'And that's why Agnes wouldn't talk to you,' whispered Prudence.

Delores nodded. 'Couldn't more like.' The skull cascaded a violet light across the room as it spun on the end of its chain. 'He thinks he can get back to the living through me *and* help himself to my necromancy while he's at it.'

Prudence watched the silver skull spin as everything fell into place. 'But you need those skills to talk to Agnes. If you don't do that…'

Delores used her other hand to stop the skull. 'Then we'll never find out the truth and Magoria wins. Oddvar, the Tolbooth… all of us are done for. I've got to get rid of Hartigan Fox and hope I can get back what he stole from me on his way through the celestial door.'

'We need more than hope,' said Prudence.

'He's still dabbling in petals and poisons, not using any of the Gifts he stole,' said Delores. 'Maybe he couldn't hang onto them when he died. I just need to make sure he dies for good this time.'

Doctor Reid gathered the sticky wrappers and plates into a pile. 'Such mortal dangers,' she said. 'I find myself wondering how Oddvar would protect you.'

'Protect us?' protested Prudence.

'All-Heavens, Prudence, it's not an insult,' said Delores. 'Thanks for worrying about us, Doctor Reid, but Hartigan Fox won't stop, not until he gets what he wants, and you can't protect us against Magoria either, not anymore.'

Doctor Reid stopped what she was doing. 'Whatever do you mean?'

'She knows about the medicine,' said Prudence, looking away. 'She's coming for you too.'

Doctor Reid took a deep breath, then said, 'It was my choice to give you the medicine, Prudence, and I'm glad I did. What we need now is a plan. Start by telling me more about this Agnes character.' She passed the plates to Delores and nodded towards the small kitchen behind the bookshelves. Delores let the pendant drop against her chest. Its weight dragged against her neck, distracting her from all thoughts of how it could be destroyed.

As Delores sorted through the plates and packaging, there was a thunderous knock on the underside of the trap door leading to the apartment. A low-pitched, resonant voice boomed its way into the room through the tiny spaces between the wood.

'Doctor Ernaline Grace Reid, I demand you open this door in the name of the High Council.'

Everyone froze. Another thunderous rap and they jumped into action. Delores dropped what she was carrying and turned back towards the others, but Doctor Reid was swiftly across the room, leaning against the bookshelves with all her might, pushing them closed. Delores was sealed in the darkness of the kitchenette, too stunned to react. She felt Prudence reaching inside her mind. *Stay hidden. We can't save the Tolbooth if they take you as well.*

Delores pressed her ear against the edges of the books that now formed a wall between her and the commotion. After more banging and shouting there was a pause followed by the sound of the trap door being pulled open and falling against the floor. Delores tried to count the footsteps, work out how many people had come up the ladder, but it was impossible. When the room fell silent, she heard Doctor Reid say, 'Prudence, don't. They'll hurt you if you try anything. They will have been very well briefed,' followed by a heart-broken, 'Findo, did you betray us?'

Findo didn't answer. Delores hoped it was because his shame had made him spontaneously combust. 'There's one missing, Commander Casparij,' he muttered. 'The Mackenzie girl. She must be here somewhere.'

'*Delores*,' said Doctor Reid, 'is running an errand at Surgeons' Hall. She's collecting some books for me.'

'Silence,' yelled the booming voice, who Delores assumed was Commander Casparij. 'Doctor Reid, you and all souls present are to be delivered into the custody of Inquisitor Jepp at the Tolbooth Book Store, where you will be held until morning. Thereafter, you will be transported to the prisons of the North for further … examination. May the Heavens have mercy on you. As for you, Findo Gast, if you have messed up our orders in any way, you can forget ever seeing your family again. The Gathering has been called.'

Delores felt her fingernails break the tender skin in the centre of her palms as she listened to the commotion that followed.

She bit back her tears as Bartleby howled at his new chains, but not as loudly as whoever was doing the shackling. Delores took some satisfaction in knowing Bartleby must have got one good bite in before he was taken. She risked sliding a slender volume from the shelf, allowing her a slither of light without being seen.

Doctor Reid was buttoning Elijah's coat with a calm confidence, brushing his hair back from his face and wiping his tears. She spoke softly to Commander Casparij, but he wagged his finger at her saying something about being immune to beguilers. Delores' attention switched to Bartleby as he writhed and snarled at some unfortunate subordinate in a much plainer version of Magoria's black and grey clothing. Delores couldn't quite see, but there was something familiar about the movement of the subordinate as they pulled their hand away from Bartleby's snapping jaws and pushed a long stray curl back from their face. A dark glimmer of recognition too horrible to consider flickered briefly before being extinguished by what Delores witnessed next; Prudence S-Dottir motionless amongst the chaos, unable for the first time in her life, to cast an illusion that would save their world and everyone in it.

24

Findo was the last to leave. He paused, looking around the empty room. Delores held her breath, as Findo's eyes came to rest on the bookshelves. She realised he must know the apartment, would have been shown the same kindnesses that Doctor Reid had shown her. The agony of not pushing that bookshelf open right there and then, leaping screaming from it, clawing at his stupid face was almost too much to bear. Findo took a step towards the bookshelf and tilted his head to one side. Delores hoped and prayed that he couldn't see the missing book. Thankfully, its neighbour had already toppled across the space. He was about to take another step closer when there was a shout from below the stairs. Findo turned down the stepladder and pulled the trap door closed behind him, but not without another backward glance at Delores' hiding place.

When she was sure they'd all left the building, Delores turned her back against the shelf and pushed. It pivoted easily and she stumbled back into the room. Doctor Reid's powdery scent still hung in the air, mixed with the sweetness of the cakes and biscuits they had eaten. The fire spat and crackled inside the stove and the world turned easily, as if nothing had happened.

The book of newspaper clippings lay open on Doctor Reid's desk. There were some new additions waiting to be stuck in: a photograph of a young woman and the story of how Hartigan Fox had been caught; *The necromancer, Imogen Parks-Burgh* it said, *had been at the ball, accompanied by the now infamous detective, Diligence Mackenzie.*

'Mackenzie?' whispered Delores. 'Well, OK then.'

It seemed Diligence's Gifts included divination much like Gabriel, catching flashes of the future from a touch of the hand. They'd turned their Gifts towards solving crimes, suspicious of Hartigan since the unexplained deaths of Edinburgh Paranormals began, piecing clues together until they led all the way back to his door. All it took was one simple touch when Hartigan risked removing a glove to add a reduction of hound's tooth petals to Imogen's drink. Diligence saw everything he'd done, everything he planned to do.

'Wow,' said Delores, '...chased to St. Anthony's chapel by the crowd of partygoers... *Officially,* she read, *Fox fell to his death from the chapel ruins perched high on the hill. However, it is rumoured that not just the living were present on that fateful Halloween night. The ghostly hands of his victims, known locally as The Five, are said to have reached through the veil that separates the living from the dead and pushed him screaming from the edge of the chapel to the path far below. At subsequent Halloweens, the spirits of The Five are said to dance in celebration amongst the ruins of the chapel.*

Delores thought back to what Sweet Shop Esme had told her. The story of The Five wasn't simple urban legend; it had leaked between their two worlds.

A report nestling beneath this one gave Delores the shivers. There was a photograph of two men carrying a stretcher covered in canvas, the bulk of a body beneath it: one man short and froggish, the other tall and ungainly. Guillemot and Bombina. Much younger, but unmistakable. Her hand drifted to the skull pendant. 'So much for honest traders.'

The cracking of wood inside the stove broke Delores' concentration.

Fire could be the answer.

If the pendant was silver, it should melt, hopefully

destroying the link between Hartigan and the living world. What she wasn't so sure of was whether he would take what he'd stolen from her with him, along with all hopes of speaking to Agnes, but like she told Doctor Reid, Hartigan Fox would never stop. He would always be waiting outside for her and The Five would become Six after all.

Delores took a thick glove from next to the stove and opened its door. The heat blasted her face, but her hand felt achingly cold as she took the chain from around her neck. She turned the pendant to look into its empty eye sockets and noticed the line around the skull and a hinge. She flipped the top of the skull open and was hit by Hartigan's special scent. There was some blackened gunk inside, the remains of his murderous potion. She snapped it shut and flung it into the fire.

At first the flames rose and hissed. Delores was sure the silver skull would melt. That Hartigan would be gone. Her excitement grew with the flames as she imagined her powers returning, how she would run full speed back to the Tolbooth. She'd find Agnes and… The floor vibrated under her and as the flames turned black, doubts gripped Delores' insides. What if her Gift didn't find its way back on its own? What if she needed to *take* it back? If she destroyed the skull without Hartigan being there…

'No, no, no!' she shouted. She reached for the stove door but it rattled furiously on its hinges and its feet juddered against the hearth as if it might rip itself from the chimney.

Delores stumbled back, landing hard on the floor. The vibrations grew stronger. Books flew from the shelves; the writing desk fell on its side and the glass apothecary bottles exploded one by one. Delores put her hands over her head and curled into a ball. With each small explosion, she could hear a deep roar building, but she couldn't work out where it was coming from, if it was inside the room or outside the balcony window, in the foundations of the building or inside her own head. She screamed as the balcony window shattered, sending glass flying across the room. The stove door sprung from its hinges and a blast of freezing wind crashed through the broken windows and smothered the flames.

Everything was silent apart from a soft whistling as a wind swirled around her, scattering papers before leaving the way it came.

Delores ran to the balcony. A tall figure disappeared into the shadows, waiting. The troll cross had kept him outside, but Hartigan Fox's reach was longer than she'd expected.

Delores knew before she got to the stove that the

pendant had not been destroyed, otherwise how could Hartigan be laughing at her from the courtyard below. Part of her was relieved, but she was still trapped with no chance of getting back to the Tolbooth. Or Agnes.

The sounds of the City rushed back in through the shattered balcony windows, but this time with added sirens and wailing security alarms. Delores sat cross legged on the floor, her head in her hands. She pulled at the longer curls on the top of her head and traced the ridges of her skull beneath the close-cropped sides. She whispered the names of the bones as she touched them, *parietal, temporal* and *occipital,* soothing sounds that calmed her thoughts. There had to be some small clue in everything that had happened. Delores reached for the last of Esme's sweets in her pocket. Her hand trembled as she popped it into her mouth. As the sweet dissolved, she felt calmer, clearer. Her thoughts ran to Esme's shop, to the pumpkins and jelly spiders, about how safe it had all seemed, how wonderful it would be to be back there.

Pumpkins.

Halloween.

That's tonight she thought. *The anniversary of the Halloween ball.*

The tower card from Gabriel's tarot flashed

through her mind. The man falling. Could it have meant Hartigan being pushed from St Anthony's chapel to his death? The chapel ruin did have a tower, kind of.

The calmer Delores felt, the more she could see the pieces of the story move towards each other. She crawled to the stove. The silver skull lay blackened against a white crust of ashes already cold from the freakish wind that extinguished the flames. She took the skull in her hand, rubbing greasy soot away from one of the sockets with her thumb and wondered if it was possible to outrun the dead, to outrun Hartigan Fox, and reach the ruins of St Anthony's chapel before he caught her one final time. Hartigan wasn't going to let her destroy it, so maybe there was another way to remove the pendant from the living world. Could she pass it into the hands of the dead, ask them to carry it back across the veil with them? It wouldn't exist in this life anymore so maybe, just *maybe*, neither would Hartigan Fox. He would be ripped from existence along with his pendant, swallowed by the dark with nothing left to tether him.

There was one nagging doubt Delores couldn't silence. It seemed the story of The Five was true, but what if their celebratory dance wasn't? Stories got added to over time, as they passed from person to person. What if the only thing that waited for Delores at St Anthony's Chapel was darkness?

Delores put the chain back over her head and stretched out the vertebrae in her neck. In the absence of a better plan, it was a risk she had to take. The clues to bringing Magoria down lay with the ghostly remains of Agnes Jepp and the only way to speak to Agnes was for Delores to take back her necromancy. There was no way round it; Hartigan Fox had to go, and Delores had to be right next to him when he did, ready to snatch her Gift back.

'Time to finish your game of tig, Mr Fox,' she said, 'and I guess I'm still it.'

26

Delores hovered in the doorway of the Writers' Museum, searching the shadows for signs of Hartigan. The windows of the buildings that surrounded the courtyard had been blown out, the same as Doctor Reid's apartment. The spaces inside lit up and went dark again as the people inside found torches and candles to guide them out onto the main street. A blue pulsating light from an emergency vehicle parked on the other side of the archway cast strange shadows across the courtyard and the crackling voice of an emergency responder could be heard on a police radio. It never ended well when the Paranormal and Normal worlds collided. Delores knew there would be repercussions, but for now her focus had to be getting the skull pendant to St Anthony's Chapel and hopefully into the ghostly hands of The Five.

A police officer strode under the archway, leaning back as she tried to slow an eager German shepherd dog that strained at its lead. The dog's barks blasted upwards, bouncing off the tall buildings surrounding them.

As the officer scanned the area, the dog grew increasingly frantic, desperate to reach something in the corner of the courtyard diagonally opposite Delores' hiding place. The police officer spoke into her radio as she was pulled closer by the dog. Two steps more and her radio failed. She took a torch from a pocket on her police vest and shone it into the corner. As a sweep of light washed across the dark space, the dog's barking reached ear-shattering levels. Delores felt her breath catch in her chest as the officer's torch lit up the grim features of Hartigan Fox. His centre was solid and detailed, and his eager, greedy eyes illuminated the empty sockets of his mask, but the edges of his body wavered.

'Guess your little temper tantrum cost you more than you expected,' whispered Delores.

The police officer looked straight at Hartigan and saw nothing. When the dog pulled her one step closer, it was the torch's turn to fail. The blue light from the emergency vehicle briefly illuminated Hartigan, and he wasn't moving.

Delores could hardly dare believe her luck. Was spooky old Hartigan Fox scared of dogs? She edged out of the doorway. The officer was distracted, tapping her torch against her leg whilst hanging on to the screeching dog's lead. Delores took the pendant by the chain and held it up to catch the blue light, making sure that Hartigan saw it. One step ahead of him, all the way into the hands of The Five. That's all she needed.

'You want to play?' she said. 'Then let's play.'

Delores slipped silently around the walls of the courtyard, keeping to the darkest shadows, until she reached the entry. She wouldn't have much of a head start but the run to the parkland below St Anthony's Chapel was a straight mile downhill, and she wanted Hartigan to be so caught up in the game, he wouldn't realise what she was up to. Until it was too late.

As Delores ran out of Ladystairs Close, a heart-breaking yelp from the dog and the frantic cries of the police officer told Delores the chase was on.

Delores glanced over her shoulder as she ran, bumping into people, breathlessly apologising. Some yelled at her, a couple lashed out with shopping bags, one even gave a quick shove back, but she didn't care. Delores needed to know that Hartigan was following her.

Anything beyond an arm's length was space enough, a few centimetres beyond the grasp of his polished nails and his creamy white fingertips. She needed him to be near enough that he believed he could reach out and grab her. She needed him to be too taken up with the chase to plot ambushes, but for all Delores knew, the Bòcain could show up anywhere they wanted. She glanced into each darkened passageway as she ran past, checking for Hartigan, telling herself that he wouldn't be able to resist the challenge she'd thrown at him in Ladystairs Close.

Delores' head was pounding, and her legs were heavy with the effort of running on an empty tank. When she turned her head again, she lost her balance. She tripped over a bagpiper's collecting box, sending coins skittering across the pavement onto the road. She landed with a smack, rolling over quickly to look back through the crowds. Couples were parting hands, wondering why, and groups were dividing as a dark nothing moved between them. A small child dressed as a pumpkin was knocked to the ground, crying as their Halloween treats spilled from their bucket into the gutter.

The piper helped Delores to her feet, thanking the passers-by who regathered his money and righted his collecting box. 'You OK?' he asked.

Delores watched the dark nothing for a few seconds as it began to take shape. The outline of its mask was silhouetted by the bright city lights as it glanced from side-to-side, searching. Then it stopped. It was looking right at her. 'Oh yeah,' Delores said to the piper, 'more than OK.' She tapped the piper's hand in thanks and ran.

There was no need to glance back now. Delores knew that Hartigan was close behind. It rekindled a childish nightmare where something is reaching out from the deep-dark to grab you, of a storm looming when you don't know how to get home.

Car horns blasted Delores out of her thoughts as she ran through a pedestrian crossing, her breath burning in her chest. She glanced at the shop windows and the glass rippled as something moved along close behind her.

Delores could hear the pounding of her heart in her ears, the slapping of her boots against the pavement and a second set of footsteps. The City noises had slipped away. He was close.

As she saw the Tolbooth Clock a little further down the hill, Delores felt the collar of her coat being flicked backwards, the scrape of a fingernail against her neck. She willed her legs to reach a little further, to lengthen her stride just enough to keep her beyond

Hartigan's fingertips, but her body had no extra to give. A few more steps and she'd be at the Tolbooth. She'd be able to take shelter, the troll cross she'd drawn there should protect her, but then she'd be caught by Magoria's henchmen, and all would be lost anyway. Maybe if she could just touch the troll cross, stop Hartigan in his tracks while she caught her breath. It might only work for a moment, but a moment was all she needed.

Pushed on by a tiny surge of hope, Delores felt a gap opening and Hartigan's fingernail drifting away from her neck. She ducked under the Book Store window and was reaching for the troll cross next to the door, palm outstretched, when a hand grabbed her shoulder, spinning her round. A human, very much alive hand. Findo Gast loomed over her. 'Well, look who it is!'

Findo shoved her hard onto her back, but the rage Delores felt from the look on his treacherous face powered a well-aimed kick to his shin. Findo screamed in pain but as Delores was almost to her feet, he grabbed her by the shoulders and flung her against the side of a big glossy black van parked on the curb. The van rattled and something or someone inside roared.

'Cook?' screamed Delores. Her fury turned back

to Findo. 'How could you,' she yelled in his face, trying to get her hands close enough to claw his eyes out. Then her body went slack and Findo looked at her, puzzled.

'Findo,' she whispered, 'you have to let me go. Now. I'm begging you for your own sake.'

Findo snorted, bemused at first, then a little afraid. He followed Delores' gaze over his shoulder. 'There's nothing there,' he said, turning back. He tightened his grip on her shoulders.

'Oh, Findo,' Delores whispered.

A creamy white hand tipped with slender black nails rested on Findo's shoulder and the ice-blue eyes of Hartigan Fox peered at Delores from behind him, flickering to the pendant around her neck. Every part of his face was outlined in sharp detail; blue-grey lips pulled into a thin smile, waxy skin that stretched over moving jawbone, and thick curls that grazed the top of his mask moving lightly in the growing wind. He was ready to take the last of her Gift and only Findo Gast stood between them.

Findo turned white, and crystals of frost grew on his eyelashes and lips. Delores felt the cold of his hands seep through her sleeves, then Findo let go of her. His knees buckled and as he dropped slowly to the floor. Delores dropped with him, using him for cover as she scrambled under the van. She lay there in the dirt and the oil and the wet, panting, waiting. She looked towards the curb. The slither of light from the street had been blocked by Hartigan's boots. There was a pause, a swish of his coat as he knelt. He knew Delores was there. Her timing had to be perfect. She had to escape but she needed Hartigan to follow. As his long white fingers reached for her coat, Delores scrambled away, scuffing across the ground and out the other side of the van. She ran towards Holyrood park, and the chapel that perched above it as if Hell was after her and if Hell was Hartigan Fox, she really hoped that it stayed close behind.

27

When Delores reached Holyrood Park, the Fire Festival was in full flow. The freezing Halloween night vibrated with deep, resonating drums and high-pitched whistles, and the light from the blazing torches held by dancers cast the hills behind them into darkness. Delores tried to pick out the edge of the chapel against the skyline, but it was impossible. She knew it was there, she just had to believe that the spirits of The Five would be there too.

'Come on, come on,' she whispered. 'Just a sign that I'm not completely crazy.'

For a fleeting moment, a ribbon of light danced around the edges of the ruined chapel walls, lighting up the space behind it with green, violet and white light. The chapel looked higher and bleaker than she remembered. Her stomach churned at the steep drop below it. The lights flickered like a guttering candle and Delores prayed they would be back when she needed them.

Delores was forced to slow down to a walk-trot-walk as she weaved her way through the ambling crowds. She could only hope that they had the same slowing effect on Hartigan. The cold was seeping through the soles of her boots and her hands stung raw in the biting Edinburgh wind but at least there was a constant supply of Halloween candy available. Almost every child was carrying an orange and black bucket rammed to the top with goodies: such easy pickings. She bit the head from a jelly snake that she'd liberated from one of the buckets and felt the rush of sugar moving her onwards.

Delores stepped into the procession of performers, using them for cover as she headed for the start of the path up to the chapel, but the throng of bodies and shadows were confusing. She inhaled the festival's delicious scents of burning wood, incense, and rich earth, constantly checking for signs of Hartigan.

Within a heartbeat of thinking of him, the raucous sounds of the festival dimmed. Delores searched the spaces between the swirling, dancing bodies as the seasonal smells were replaced by cooler, sharper ones.

An acrobat wearing antlers was spun from a one-arm handstand to the ground; a dancer with ram's horns and a ragged fleece was knocked into a stilt walker who teetered and toppled, scattering his juggling torches amongst the surrounding performers. A dark shadow rose amongst the growing pandemonium, marching relentlessly forward.

Delores dipped back and grabbed one of the scattered torches. She shoved her way through the last of the dancers, relieved as her feet hit the boggy ground that marked the start of the path upwards to the chapel ruins, but her relief dimmed with every step she took. What if this ended with her own death at the hands of Hartigan Fox? She shuddered as she imagined being the next one to fall from the chapel, her body eventually being carried away by Bombina and Guillemot on their canvas-covered stretcher.

The torch flickered and faltered as Delores picked her way around the jutting stones and freezing puddles along the path. She tried to gain a bit of speed, but the ground was getting steeper. She stopped and looked behind her, waiting for a glimpse of Hartigan's masked face, the suggestion of his long coat moving amongst the shadows, but she couldn't see anything in the darkest deep-night black.

She sniffed the air again. If her eyes couldn't help her, she'd use her other senses but the smell of the paraffin from the torch was smothering everything.

Delores turned back to the climb, sucking in the cold air as her heart beat faster and faster, her ears prickling, scanning for sounds. There was a crunching of a boot on loose stones behind her. Then another, getting closer. She waved the torch all around her, spinning, searching for Hartigan, but the light blinded her to anything that moved in the darkness. He had to be there somewhere. He wouldn't have lost track of her and there was no way he would have given up. That left one unthinkable possibility. He'd figured it out. Hartigan had realised he wasn't chasing Delores; it was Delores that was reeling him in.

The wind caught the edge of her coat and the bell inside the silver ball she carried in her pocket tinkled. She thought of Oddvar sitting next to the fire, Oddvar who'd only known her for a few months but was prepared to die to protect her. Now, alone on the bitterly bleak hillside, it was time for Delores to pay him back. Magoria's downfall was sure to be sweet, and making sure Hartigan was gone for ever would be the icing on the cherry fondant biscuit.

Delores held the pendant up, making sure the skull caught the light from the torch as it spun. 'You want the last little scraps of my Gift?' she shouted. 'Well, you better come and get it while you've got the chance. I've got your precious pendant, and I am going to send it from this world into the next. And you will be GONE. FOREVER!'

The torchlight flickered, the flame burning lower beneath a gentle shush of smoke, and through it, Delores saw something move. She walked backwards a few steps, her fear almost unbearable, like the moment before a jump-scare in a film when you know something is coming, you just don't know when.

Delores turned and ran. When she reached a set of higgledy steps, she knew she was near the top. She could see the chapel ahead of her, silhouetted against the city's night sky. Distant lights twinkled through the stone doorway that had once led to a tower and outlined the crumbling edge of a wall that stood perilously close to the steep drop to the loch below.

The wind whipped the longer strands of Delores' hair around her face, stealing her breath as she waited, watching the steps she'd just climbed. There was a movement deep inside the darkness, a glimpse of a bone-white hand, the flickering of two ice-blue eyes in the pitch black.

The skull spun on its chain and Delores' arm ached with its heaviness. The wind tugged at her silently now, no more howls and whistles. There was a scrambling of loose stones, something rushing at her. Hartigan was coming.

As she turned to run the last few steps to the chapel ruins, there was a flickering of light through the stone doorway, but it quickly dissolved into the night.

'Come back!' Delores shouted, her heart sinking. She felt something reach out from the darkness behind her, but as she glanced over her shoulder, her boot hit a rock and she was catapulted forward to the ground. The torch spun away from her hand and hit the chapel wall; its dying light snuffed out. A hand grabbed Delores' ankle and dragged her back. She held on to the pendant chain and watched as the silver skull trailed through the dirt behind her.

'Help me!' screamed Delores, desperate to see the lights reignite. 'You have to help me!'

Hartigan sank his bony fingers deeper as Delores twisted round onto her back. He loomed over her, letting go of her ankle and catching hold of her coat just below her throat. He pulled her up towards him and she could see the outline of his jaw moving beneath his skin, ready to speak.

Hartigan cleared his throat and a beetle scurried across his face into the dark feathers of his mask. With a voice as dry as sandpaper, he whispered, 'Gotcha.'

Hartigan kept his eyes locked on Delores as he reached for his pocket. Delores knew what would come next and she didn't think she had the strength to resist this time. Hartigan would use those cursed petals to take what little necromancy she had left. She'd never talk to Agnes; Agnes' secrets would never be told, secrets that Obsidian seemed so sure were the key to Magoria's downfall, the key to saving her friends from the prisons of the North.

Hartigan opened his hand and blew the petals from his palm.

As they drifted around Delores' face, she could feel the bitterness of the hound's tooth orchid on her tongue. Her eyes were heavy, her head cloudy. She was forgetting. She knew she had to remember to say something, but the words were slipping away into a dream.

'Help me,' she whispered, though she no longer grasped why or who she was asking. The last tiny seed of the necromancy that she was still guarding deep inside her flared for a brief second as the words slipped from her lips. Delores heard Hartigan laugh as she drifted towards oblivion, her hand loosening its grip round something precious that she couldn't quite remember.

28

Delores had hit the ground with a damp thud. She could hear a high-pitched whistling sound, swooping over her, screeching as it got closer, then easing off again. She remembered Hartigan had been holding onto her by her coat, but when she patted around her chest, his hand was gone.

The swooping and screeching came again. Delores needed to see what was happening, but her eyes were still heavy and when she rubbed at the back of her head, it was sticky with blood. Something was tangled around the fingers of her other hand. Something heavy, something important, if only she could remember.

The screeching looped back round, but this time she heard footsteps running past her, not one person, at least three, maybe four. Delores didn't dare wish for a fifth.

She sat up too quickly. Her head was swimming and after a couple of hard blinks she could make out Hartigan's masked figure kneeling at her feet, his wraith-like fingers swatting at streams of green, white, and violet light swirling above his head.

Delores wished the noise would stop, even for a few seconds so she could make sense of everything. She closed her eyes and pressed her hands against her temples. Something hard hit her cheekbone and when she opened her eyes again, she was looking at the silver skull. Then she remembered. She had to destroy Hartigan, and she had to take her Gift back when she did.

The lights swirling around Hartigan stretched themselves out into five long, thin bodies with furious faces and their screeches sharpened to piercing screams of *Hartigan* and *Murderer.* As the five spirits pulled at his hair and his clothes, Delores' plan didn't seem so ridiculous after all.

Before Delores could call out to them, the spirits dipped and scratched at Hartigan's face like gulls, pulling at his mask until it shattered into tiny shards of brittle fabric, scattering feathers and beads at Delores' feet. She was expecting to see a monster, but under Hartigan's long-dead face were glimmers of the lonely young man in the photographs. Delores might have pitied him if he hadn't lunged at her. She could feel his hands pressing into her shoulders as she hit the ground again. The spirits of The Five regathered for their attack but Delores couldn't move. She frantically searched the ground with her hand, hoping to find a loose stone but she found something better. With a ferocious swing, she hit Hartigan with the juggler's torch, hoping his body was solid enough to feel an impact. He was only knocked backwards for an instant, but it gave Delores the chance she needed to scramble away. She leaned back against the chapel wall, catching her breath as the spirits circled for another round with Hartigan, but with each attack their light was dimming, and their screams sounded more like wind through hollow reeds.

This was not what Delores had planned. She'd begged The Five to help her, and they were, but this is not what she meant. This was not the plan.

The plan, she thought, realising she'd forgotten one of the basic rules for dealing with the dead, even the friendly ones. You must be specific.

She scrambled to her feet and held the pendant up so that the spirits could see it. 'Listen to me,' she shouted. 'This is what's keeping Hartigan anchored in the living world. Take it with you, back to the place of the peaceful dead. That's how we'll destroy him!'

Delores spun the chain, unravelling it from her hand.

The spirits stopped their attack and their faces turned towards Delores. They'd seen or heard something, she was sure of that, but she didn't know how much and if they'd understood.

The pause was enough for Hartigan to grab hold of Delores again. He dragged her from the safety of the chapel wall to the edge of the gaping fall to the loch below. One of her heels dipped over the edge and her stomach lurched, but Hartigan didn't let go. He was searching her face, looking for that last tiny seed of her necromancy. Once he had that, he would let her fall. Delores imagined burying it deeper, protecting it in a tiny precious box, but she knew she didn't have much longer.

Hartigan laughed to himself. He'd found it.

He pulled her closer and whispered, 'Farewell, Delores Mackenzie.'

'You haven't won yet,' answered Delores, as the spirits hovered silently behind Hartigan, waiting.

She smiled a Prudence-type smile, as she let the pendant drop through her fingers.

It did not hit the ground.

Hartigan Fox wailed as the pendant was swept up in a stream of lights, a mingling of hands and arms and delighted faces. His grip softened and it was his turn to look scared.

Delores shoved him and he staggered back two steps, lighter, weaker already. She grabbed hold of his lapels and spun him around towards the edge of the drop. This was it. All she wanted was enough of her Gift back to speak to Agnes. She didn't care if there was nothing left after Agnes' story was told. She'd even go back to Normal school (OK, maybe not that) but if the Tolbooth was saved she was at peace with whatever came next. She watched the spirits carry the pendant to the old chapel door. They hesitated, giving Delores the moment she needed to steady herself. She nodded and the Five stepped back through the chapel doorway, taking the pendant with them.

Delores tightened her grip on Hartigan, and she felt his arms cave under her touch. His body sagged and he looked shrunken.

'Now give me back what you took from me,' she snarled. She opened her mind and her heart, ready for that burst of energy as Hartigan inevitably disintegrated out of existence.

Hartigan's jaw wobbled as he tried to speak but nothing came out. As the last of the light faded beyond the chapel ruins, there was the cracking of brittle bones that multiplied like kindling on a log fire. With each snap, Delores felt … nothing.

Hartigan's jaw dropped into a gawp and the edges of his form flickered, but still he held on to Delores, greedily searching for the last of her necromancy.

'You cannot have it,' whispered Delores, 'and you are uninvited.'

There was a sorrowful sigh from somewhere in the hollows of Hartigan's collapsing body, but he still reached for Delores and what he thought he could take from her. The tips of his fingers grazed her cheek, and she felt his nails lift the tiniest slither of skin.

Hartigan smiled as deep down inside Delores, a light went out.

'No … no. Give it back. Give it back, NOW!' shouted Delores.

Hartigan laughed as his face cracked along his cheekbones and his blue eyes turned to pools of liquid black. A final whip-sharp snap and he shattered into an exploding mosaic of black and white pieces that whisked around the hilltop in the swirling wind.

Delores frantically grabbed at the last of the drifting pieces, hoping that the tiniest drop of her Gift was held somewhere in their fabric. She scrabbled on the ground, trying to sweep enough together to give her the power she needed to speak to Agnes, but the last earthly scraps of Hartigan Fox fizzled to nothing in her hand.

Delores had been certain that if she was there when Hartigan was defeated, her Gift would flow back to her. She'd been right about everything else, each little piece of the puzzle had convinced her she would win: Hartigan falling for her game, the five spirits, the passing of the skull through the veil. How could she have been so wrong about this one final thing?

Delores had failed.

She had failed everyone.

29

Delores watched the lights of the festival guttering to nothing far below. She staggered along the wall of the chapel and crouched down inside the old doorway. She drew her knees to her chin and pulled the collar of her coat up to protect her neck from the biting cold. She ran her hand along her collarbone, feeling for the fronds of her markings, but they were flat and smooth against her fingertips. She felt thinner on the inside, hollowed out, and wondered if her fate was sealed like it was for The Five. Would she slowly shrivel and die like they had? If that was true, she might as well surrender to Magoria and the Gathering. Her friends would know she'd failed, they might even hate her, but she couldn't let them think she'd abandoned them. Return to the Tolbooth; that's what she'd do. A few seconds rest, a chance to catch her breath, then she'd go. Delores let her head rest back against the wall, and her eyes drifted shut.

Delores woke in a panic. She had no idea how long she'd slept but it was quiet now, except for the wind softly moving through the bushes and grasses below. The stars were bright, and a gibbous moon cast a silvery light over the chapel ruins.

Bumped, bruised, and battle weary, the muscles in Delores' arms complained bitterly as she ran her fingers through her hair and rubbed the sleep from her face.

A hand settled on her shoulder.

Delores felt a gentle vibration moving through her skin and the flattened fronds of her markings rose like prickly hairs in the freezing cold.

'Whoever you are,' she said. 'You've got the wrong necromancer. This one's officially broken.'

Someone laughed softly. A laugh she recognised. It was full of warmth and love, of breakfasts at the cottage at Cramond, of happy moments Delores thought she'd released forever into the waters of the Forth on the day she was sent to the Tolbooth.

She hardly dared say the word.

'Mum?'

It couldn't be. How would her mother know where to find her?

Dread rolled through Delores' stomach. This was not the answer she'd been looking for. It was the worst of all endings.

A warm hand slipped under her chin and tilted her face gently upwards. Delores refused to look. If she didn't see her mother's face, it might not be true. The delicate perfume, run through with soft spices, told her that it was. This was her mother, and Delores knew from her touch that her mother was dead.

Magda Mackenzie kissed her daughter softly on her cheek. 'I am so sorry, my baby,' she said. 'I didn't plan to come to you like this, but I heard you calling.'

Tears slipped freely down Delores' face. 'Tell me I'm wrong, Mum,' she pleaded. 'Tell me you're alive. You have to be, or I couldn't ... he took it, my Gift, all of it, so you must be...'

'It's my Gift we're using now, my sweet.' Magda drew Delores closer, holding her head to her chest, kissing her as she wept. 'We never thought it would end this way,' she said. 'We would never choose to leave you and Delilah. Not for anything.'

'I never gave up on you,' sobbed Delores. 'Delilah though, she...'

'Hush now,' whispered Magda. 'I don't have much time. The veil is closing, calling me back. I need you to promise me something, then I'll rest easy. Forgive your sister, and never, ever give up looking for your father.'

Delores choked on her words as more tears came. 'Forgive Delilah? What for?'

She looked up at her mother, searching for answers but the warm glow from her delicately freckled face was already faltering at its edges.

'Promise me,' said Magda.

'I promise, I just don't understand.' Delores felt her mother's hold tighten around her, pressing intense warmth and light through Delores' body. She felt a tiny seed of necromancy ignite in the hollow space where her own used to be and as it bloomed into life, Magda Mackenzie faded away.

Love you, pumpkin, were the last words Delores would ever hear her mother say.

30

The clock was trying to strike midnight when Delores reached the Tolbooth. She'd almost fallen twice on her way up the Canongate. Carrying her mother's necromancy inside her was like trying to walk in someone else's boots. She hoped it would feel as much a part of her as her own Gift by the time she had to use it.

The Tavern Bòcan was in his usual spot next door, staring through the window, tapping on the glass. Delores watched him for a moment. She hadn't taken the time before to think how sad he might be, that he wanted to be with his loved ones. Maybe that was why he was still around. Delores was a little envious of his sadness though. She wanted to feel her own grief, to sob and keen and lament, but it was too big, too terrifying to let loose. Delores wasn't ready. And she had a job to do.

The black van was still parked outside the Tolbooth Book Store. *Poor Cook* thought Delores. She put her ear against the cold metal and listened to the soft rumbling inside. The van rocked as someone big turned over in their sleep, followed by some swearing in French. Cook *and* Bartleby. At least they were together. Delores hoped Bartleby had his blanket.

She reached into her inside pocket, feeling for Prudence's almost-everything key but she quickly realised that it was only good for buildings, not for vans and cars. 'We'll be back for you,' she whispered.

The Book Store was in darkness; Delores couldn't be sure who might be waiting on the other side of the door. The officers from the High Council could be inside, the ones from Doctor Reid's apartment. She thought again about the subordinate officer, the familiarity of her hair, the way she brushed it from her face in frustration when Bartleby resisted arrest. It made her sick to think about it. *Forgive your sister.* Is that what her mother had meant? Had Delilah turned traitor? She wasn't sure she could ever forgive that. Delilah and Findo would make a lovely couple; they deserved each other.

Delores tapped the palm of her hand with the key as she listened to Cook's rumbles in the van. She looked up at the kitchen window and the door at the top of the service steps.

'Worth a shot.'

The Tavern Bòcan tilted its head, listening.

'Well, that's a good sign,' said Delores. She wanted to thank him, but she still didn't know his name. Plus, he'd already turned back to stare through the window. 'I'll find out who you are one day,' said Delores. 'You deserve to be called by your name.'

The Bòcan ignored her. He was too busy lightly tapping on the glass.

At the top of the service steps, Delores felt queezy for the first time in hours. Blown against the bottom of the door and the edge of the wall were the soggy remains of Hartigan's petals. She knew they couldn't harm her now, but she still didn't want to look at them. She nudged them to one side with the toe of her boot and knelt next to the lock. She imitated Prudence's efforts with the key and after a couple of false starts, the lock clicked open.

Delores slowly opened the door, hoping that the kitchen would have been abandoned for the night. To her horror, a uniformed officer was lying on the floor, huddled up against the warm range. They pulled their thin blanket up around their shoulders as they felt a cool draft from the door, but it didn't wake them. Delores clicked the door closed behind her and crept across the kitchen and into the corridor. The fire in the dining room was still lit and cast its warm orange glow across the walls and shelves. Oddvar was exactly as they'd left him, Gabriel asleep at his feet. She crept past the closed bedroom doors and slipped up the spiral stone stairs to her room in the tower.

Prudence was awake, reading her troll book. 'What took you so long?' she asked, without looking up. Delores knew better than to expect a rapturous welcome.

'Missed you too,' said Delores. 'Thought Magoria might have you in chains by now.'

Prudence made a show of checking her wrists and arms. 'Clearly not. All the doors are locked and as you're now inside, I'm thinking you pocketed my almost-everything key at some point.'

'And you would be correct,' said Delores.

'Hmm. Gabriel left you something.'

Delores politely ignored the nest-like state of Prudence's bed, her neck to toe nightgown and stripey woollen socks. Very Un-Prudence but whatever made her comfortable these days was fine with Delores. She was just glad to see her.

Delores' bed, in contrast, had been freshly made and the quilt pulled taut. In the middle was one of

Gabriel's tarot cards. The tower. 'I'd hoped never to see that again.' She picked the card up and ran her hand over its surface.

'Is Hartigan Fox gone?' asked Prudence.

Delores nodded. 'So why this card?'

Prudence shrugged. Delores slipped the card into her back pocket and marched over to the clocktower door. The dolls were still on the step where she left them. She flipped them over one by one, lined them up and waited. The taller scraggy doll reached out and took the hand of the smallest one, pursing its rosebud lips and frowning at Delores.

'Hello again,' said Delores, smiling.

Prudence got out of bed, threw a shawl around her shoulders, and sank down next to her.

'Is it Agnes? Ouch ...what happened to your face?'

Delores put her hand up to the scratch Hartigan had made.

Prudence touched Delores' shoulder, searching inside her mind for what had happened to her since they were separated.

'Please don't,' whispered Delores. 'I'll tell you in my own time. Let's focus on Agnes.'

Prudence nodded and let go.

Delores took the almost-everything key from her pocket, but before she had chance to use it, the handle slowly turned and the door to the clocktower creaked open. A waft of stale air rushed over Delores' face as she stared up into the darkness. She handed the key to Prudence. 'Thanks for the lend. Coming?'

Prudence slow blinked at Delores.

Delores hoped that was a *yes*.

The first few steps were dark, and Delores used the edge of her boot to feel her way. Prudence grabbed the hem of Delores' coat and followed close behind. 'You know I won't be any use, right? I mean, ghosts aren't my thing.'

'Don't worry,' said Delores. 'It's great having your huge intellect along, you know, just in case.'

Halfway up the staircase, it got easier to see where they were going. An eerie light was shining in through an open door to the right.

'It's the mechanism room for the clock,' whispered Prudence. 'It's normally locked. Only the clock guy has a key. He's never been able to fix the clock though. That's why it whirrs and clunks like it does. I don't think I've ever heard it chime.'

'And you've never been tempted?' Delores asked. 'You know, to use your *special* key and go exploring?'

Prudence shuddered. 'Ughhh. As if.'

As they climbed two steps higher, Delores heard a thin, reedy voice singing a familiar nursery rhyme:

Where did you go to?
Where did you hide?

'Agnes? Is that you?' whispered Delores. The singing stopped and Delores heard someone catch their breath.

'What is going on?' whispered Prudence.

Delores shushed her and she could feel Prudence's fury simmering behind her. 'Sorry,' whispered Delores, 'but it's Agnes and I need to listen.' They stepped up another stair. The singing started again.

You're not in any wee places I tried.
No trace of footsteps,
No sight nor no sound…

It stopped. The short hairs at the base of Delores' skull bristled. She took the last two steps and put her hand on the edge of the doorway that led to the mechanism room. A girl was standing in the corner, a shadowy space where the light from the street and the clockface couldn't reach. The girl had her back to them, and looked like she was holding her hands up over her eyes. She didn't move. Delores tried a small light switch but of course it didn't work.

Delores cleared her throat, and sang the last two

lines, 'God rest you and keep you, Deep down in the ground.'

'O.K. Freaked out now,' said Prudence.

'Don't be. It's only Agnes. I think she's a simple ghost. Unlikely to hurt us.'

'Unlikely?' muttered Prudence. 'Great.'

'Coming, ready or not,' said Agnes, as she turned to face Delores. She was small, with wavy shoulder-length hair tied back from her face with a ribbon. Her face was pale and featureless, and her eyes were the typical pools of watery black. She wore a purple velvet dress that hung loose below her waist, skirting the top of her black boots.

'Hello, Agnes,' said Delores. 'Do you know who I am?'

Agnes shook her head. 'Where's my toybox? Magoria's hidden my best doll. She's mean.'

'Worse than mean,' said Delores.

Prudence squeezed her hand. 'What's going on?'

Delores put her finger to her lips. She turned her attention back to Agnes. 'Magoria's your sister, right?'

Agnes nodded. 'She pushed me into the toybox and locked me in. I fell asleep but then I couldn't breathe. It was so hot. And then … I remember the graveyard. I didn't like it. I came here to find my best doll, but they'd all been put away. I didn't like that either.'

'No,' said Delores, 'that wasn't nice. Erm … we think Magoria's been very naughty and now she wants to hurt my friends.'

'Magoria is mean,' said Agnes, starting to cry. 'It was an accident, but she didn't want to take the blame. She never took the blame. Not for anything. She hurt that boy who came to find out, the boy that could see me. She didn't like that. And then no one came. Have you seen my toybox? I think Magoria hid my best doll.'

Agnes turned back to the wall and started to count. By the time she got to five, her outline was wavering, and the colour of her dress was fading.

'Damn,' said Delores. 'I think we're losing her for tonight.'

'Do something,' said Prudence. 'Bring her back. Tonight's all we've got.'

'I'm aware, OK?' Delores tried reaching out to Agnes, but her necromancy felt unfamiliar, not part of her fabric yet. Meanwhile, Agnes was fading into the wall. There had to be a clue in what Agnes was saying. 'Hey Prudence… did you see a toybox anywhere? It must be pretty big. Probably one of those old trunk things. Something you could … suffocate in.'

'There's a storeroom on the other side of the stairs,' said Prudence. 'What if I find it, though? I mean, is it OK to look inside?'

Delores sighed. 'Agnes isn't in there if that's what you're worried about. She remembers being in the graveyard. We're looking for her best doll.'

'What will *that* look like?'

'Old? Expensive? Obsidian said the Jepps were an *influential family*. I read that as filthy rich.'

Delores heard Prudence patter off into the next room. It was surprising how cooperative she was when things got spooky.

'Agnes?' called Delores, gently. 'Can you remember what happened to the boy? What was he called?'

'Five, six, seven...' Her voice was breaking apart.

'His name, Agnes?'

Prudence dashed back into the mechanism room, waving a porcelain-faced doll in a long grey dress. 'It was at the bottom of an old trunk like you said. Under a load of other stuff wrapped in a drawing. Bit dirty but definitely expensive.'

Delores took the doll. She hated dolls. Especially other people's. 'Is this the one?' she asked, but Agnes' ghost was just a shimmer of light against the wall.

'Is it working?' Prudence asked.

Delores shook her head. She carried the doll to Agnes' spot against the wall. As she got closer, she caught tiny shimmers of Agnes' boots, of the edge of her dress drifting in and out of the bricks. And soft, rapid breaths.

Delores sat cross legged on the floor and started to braid the doll's gruesomely real hair, hoping there weren't any spiders in it. 'Look Agnes,' she said. 'I found your doll. The one you're looking for. Your best…'

Agnes snapped back in sharp focus. She spun around from the wall, her face and jaw stretched thin with fury. The air filled with static as she screamed like only a small child can, her arms rigid by her sides.

Delores dropped the doll and scrambled backwards to the centre of the room. 'I'm sorry, I'm sorry,' she said. 'We just want to help.'

'What's happening?' shouted Prudence. 'I can feel something weird in the air.'

'It's fine, it's fine.' But Delores wasn't sure it was.

Agnes stopped screaming as quickly as she started and sank down next to the doll. She tried to touch it, but her hand went straight through. 'Hello Mirabelle,' she said, glaring first at the new braid and then at Delores.

Agnes' *simple* ghost felt a lot more dangerous than Delores had bargained for. 'The boy who came looking,' she said cautiously, 'what was he called?'

'I don't like you anymore,' said Agnes. 'You ruined Mirabelle's hair. I don't want to talk to you. Go. Away!'

'If you want Magoria to be punished,' said Delores, 'I need to know about the boy.'

Agnes narrowed her eyes. 'I don't like you anymore,' she repeated. 'Magoria is mean. Someone should tell on Magoria. Have you seen my toybox?'

'No, no, no!' said Delores. She was starting to panic. If Agnes was slipping back into a loop, she could disappear any minute. 'I'm truly sorry for touching Mirabelle,' she said. 'I'm begging you, tell me his name and I'll make sure Magoria gets in trouble.'

It felt like an eternity before Agnes finally said, 'Thomas drew my picture. He wrote down what I told him. Magoria pushed him down the stairs. Someone should tell on Magoria. She is mean. She's hidden my best doll. Have you seen my toybox?' Agnes stood and turned to the wall, putting her hands over her eyes.

'He drew your picture?' Delores spun round, checking out Prudence's hands. 'The drawing? Prudence, have you got the drawing?' Prudence dashed back into the other room and Delores could hear her rummaging amongst the boxes again.

'Got it!' shouted Prudence. 'Oh, there's writing on the back.'

'Coming ready or not,' sang Agnes as she faded into the shadows. When Delores looked, Mirabelle was gone too.

31

Magoria Jepp woke at four in the morning. That would be the only normal part of her day.

Delores, Prudence and Gabriel were already at the dining-room table, along with Doctor Reid and Elijah who'd both been locked in Oddvar's room. Prudence soon had them out of there.

The piece of paper from the toybox took pride of place in the centre of the table. It was crinkled but newly smoothed out, freshly read by everyone assembled. The guard in the kitchen slept soundly on, assisted by one of Doctor Reid's elixirs.

Magoria covered her shock well. 'Miss Mackenzie,' she said, 'how reckless of you to join us. The transport leaves at 5 am for the northern coast, then onwards to Norway. I'm sure we can squeeze you in. And how are you out of your room, Ernaline Reid?'

'And a good morning to you Magoria,' said Ernaline, 'and its *Doctor* Reid.'

Magoria bristled and yelled Findo's name. The door to Gabriel's bedroom flew open and a bleary-eyed Findo Gast staggered out. Delores felt relieved to see him. Then furious to see him.

'Traitor!' she snarled. She could see the nightmares wrought on his face, the dark circles under his eyes. Hartigan Fox had been good for one thing at least.

'Go and fetch Commander Casparij and his assistant from the Tavern rooms,' said Magoria. 'They'll be awake by now and I'm sure they can forgo breakfast.' Her eyes flickered to the piece of paper on the table. 'What's that?'

'You're the Inquisitor,' said Delores. 'You figure it out.'

Magoria went to snatch up the paper, but Gabriel whipped it from beneath her fingers.

'I can *make* you give it to me, young man,' hissed Magoria.

'Go on,' said Gabriel. 'I dare you.'

'Gabriel, don't,' whispered Prudence reaching for his hand, but it was too late. Magoria was already probing around inside his head. This time, Gabriel didn't fight. He didn't shut down. He let Magoria peek at the evidence they had against her.

Magoria blanched.

'Give it to her,' said Delores. 'It doesn't matter anyway. We've all seen it.'

Magoria snatched the piece of paper. She ran her hand over the picture of Agnes, then flipped it over to read the notes on the back. Her hands were shaking as she folded the paper over and over into a tiny square.

'You think this will save you?' Her voice was as shaky as her hands. 'Paper is easily destroyed.'

'But we are not,' said Doctor Reid. 'We have all read it. If another inquisitor looked in our minds, they would see the truth.'

'Only that my sister died by accident,' said Magoria.

'Oh, about that,' said Delores. 'I've spoken to Agnes' ghost and that little encounter is firmly embedded up here.' She tapped her temple.

'And here,' said Prudence, copying Delores' actions.

'Oh, and here,' said Gabriel.

'We know about Thomas, the necromancer,' said Delores. 'The one who spoke to Agnes' ghost. We know it was your fault she died and that you pushed poor Thomas down the stairs to cover it up. That's why Oddvar would never have necromancers here before me, because of what happened to Thomas.'

'And if you take your findings to the High Council,'

said Prudence, 'or the Psychic Adjustment Council, or any other council you can think of, and tell them anything about *any* of us—'

'No one will listen to a trio of whiny teenagers,' laughed Magoria, but Delores caught a nervous edge to that laugh, and when she looked at Prudence and Gabriel, she knew they'd heard it too.

'You don't sound so sure, Magoria,' said Doctor Reid. 'And even if you are correct, I'll simply insist on a fresh interrogation. Whoever investigates their minds next will see that they are telling the truth, and you will be finished.'

'They'll still be in prison,' snapped Magoria. 'And so will you. A shapeshifter and her accomplices are quite a prize. It might even buy me some bargaining room.'

There was the sound of boots on the stairs and the gruff rumblings of Commander Casparij, furious at being disturbed.

'I guess you've got a few seconds to decide if it's worth your own freedom,' said Delores.

As Commander Casparij rounded the stairwell, Delores got her first full look at his assistant.

It was Delilah.

Her own sister.

Delores remembered their mother's words, the forgiveness she'd promised, but this betrayal felt beyond forgiveness.

Delilah met her eye and shook her head. 'It's not what you…'

Delores looked away.

'What in all-Heavens is going on?' growled Commander Casparij. His napkin was still tucked in his uniform jacket and a dollop of egg yolk was hardening on his chin. He pulled up the last chair. 'May I get some coffee at least? Black if you please.'

Prudence smirked. 'You could if you hadn't locked up Cook.'

She looked surprised when Commander Casparij nodded in agreement. 'A tactical error. Now, Inquisitor Jepp, what is so important that my breakfast is ruined?'

All eyes were on Magoria. There was silence except for the whistling sound of Magoria breathing rapidly through her tiny nose, lips pressed so tightly together that they were almost white. Delores couldn't tear her eyes from Magoria's hand as she flipped the small square of paper between her fingers like a playing card. Finally, Magoria Jepp tucked the folded drawing and its damning words into her hip pocket.

'Enough of this silence,' barked Commander

Casparij. 'I am still without breakfast and most certainly without patience.'

Magoria cleared her throat. 'My Inquisition has proven to be … flawed, Commander. It appears I am unwell. It has caused me to see things that perhaps … are not there.'

Commander Casparij didn't move. He looked wide-eyed at Magoria. 'Inquisitor Jepp, either this is a joke, or someone has bewitched you. For you own sake, it had better be bewitchment.'

Magoria's pallid cheeks flushed pink. 'I can assure you it is neither.'

Commander Casparij put his head in his hands. 'And the rift in the Paranormal Sphere? The one you insisted on investigating personally? That has kept you here all these months at GREAT cost to the High Council?'

Delores shifted uneasily in her chair. Would Magoria choose their downfall over her own freedom?

Commander Casparij slammed his hand down on the table, startling everyone. 'Answer!' he yelled.

Magoria hung her head. 'An anomaly,' she whispered, her voice barely audible. 'I will make my report and my apologies to the High Council in person.'

'Tja!' spat Commander Casparij. 'And what of this mess you have made? What of the students? The resident Uncle is extremely unwell, no doubt made worse by your *flawed inquisition.*'

Although Magoria's head was still bowed, Delores saw her smirk.

'Quite right, Commander,' said Magoria. 'In the absence of a responsible Uncle, it would be protocol to send them elsewhere. They would have to be separated of course. I wouldn't want my mistakes to cause problems for other placements. I believe the Uncles in Turku and Sigtuna have vacancies.'

'Commander,' said Doctor Reid. 'Do not allow Inquisitor Jepp to compound her mistakes with cruelty. The students have formed deep bonds. They rely on each other.'

Before the Commander could answer, he was distracted by a shadow that moved across the table. It warmed itself briefly in front of the fire before taking hold of Oddvar's hand. Oddvar's fingers twitched in response and the shadow moved back towards the stairway to greet its master with a flourish.

'Uncle Obsidian,' said Delores.

'Uncle Obsidian,' groaned Prudence, checking her neck for feathers.

Commander Casparij stood and gave a sharp bow. 'I am honoured, sir. May I introduce my assistant, Delilah Mackenzie?'

Delilah stepped forward and Obsidian held out his hand. As Delilah took it, Delores caught a fleeting exchange between the two of them. They'd already met.

'Ms Mackenzie. More charming than your younger sister, I hope.'

Delores glowered at Obsidian. Why was he lying? And how did he know Delilah?

Obsidian let Delilah's hand drop and Delores saw the edge of the note that had been passed between them.

'I will stand in as Uncle,' said Obsidian to the room. 'Only until Oddvar recovers of course. There is no need to close the Tolbooth. All-Heavens, Ms Jepp, is that really you? I haven't seen you since … what was it now, oh yes, since poor Thomas Lafferty took a tumble. Shame we never got to the bottom of that.' He stared at Magoria, daring her to respond.

Magoria nodded a curt but respectful greeting. 'Uncle,' she said. 'How delightful. Would you please excuse me, I must pack.'

What followed was chaotic and hard for Delores to recall in any particular order. Magoria made her exit wrapped in furs, her head held high. Findo Gast carried her bags and was never seen in Edinburgh again, neither was his family. The Cormicans showed up before dawn to collect Elijah, and Ainsley wept as she swept the exhausted boy into her arms. Even Balgair looked relieved to see him.

Obsidian shooed everyone back as, with Doctor Reid's permission, he tucked Oddvar's blanket around him and carried him with great dignity to his room. Oddvar's eyes didn't open, but they flickered, and his hand grasped the sleeve of Obsidian's coat.

Prudence and Gabriel were ordered by Commander Casparij to retrieve Bartleby from the van; they were the only ones other than Delores that the furious gargoyle wouldn't bite. There was a rumpus in the kitchen as the sleeping officer was thrown out of the service door, followed by the comforting sound of pans clattering onto the range.

That left Delores and Delilah alone in front of the fire.

Delilah wrapped her arms around Delores, holding her tight. 'Mum's dead,' she whispered.

Delores tried to pull away. 'I know. I've seen her.'

Delilah stepped back, still holding Delores by the shoulders. 'What? When? I didn't want you to find out like that.'

'But you couldn't have found a way to tell me?'

'I'm so sorry, Delores. I wanted to but—'

'But what? What else could have been soooooo important? Tell me what happened to Mum. Now!'

Delilah checked over her shoulder. 'I don't know. I only know she died. I'm trying to find out, but word is that Dad's still alive, still locked up somewhere. That's what I'm doing in this awful uniform; I'm playing a part. Can't you see that?'

'No. No, I can't,' snapped Delores. 'You just stood there while my friends were taken prisoner, even Bartleby. I'm glad he bit you. I hope he's given you some weird gargoyle disease.'

'And I felt wretched about all of it.' Delilah took a breath. 'Our people are working to stop these Gatherings, trying to end this cruelty. You of all people should see how important that is.'

Delores pulled her head back. 'What do you mean "our people"?'

Delores' collar was pulled to one side in her efforts to get away from her sister.

Delilah let go. 'Those marks,' she gasped.

Delores put her hand up to her neck. 'What about them? Going to report it to the Commander? Or your new best pal, Obsidian? Don't think I didn't notice you two were all cosy. You must think we're idiots. And now you're going to leave me with him. He hates Prudence and clearly thinks I'm a HUGE problem. Thanks a lot.'

'It might not look like it,' said Delilah, 'but he's on

our side. And those marks you have? Dad has them too. I didn't know about them until…'

Delilah jumped when Commander Casparij yelled up the stairs that it was time to leave. She pulled Delores back into a hug. 'Say the word *disruptor* to Obsidian when you're alone … and trust him.'

Before Delores could ask her anything else, Delilah was gone.

The clock in the tower struck five. As the clear chimes echoed through the Tolbooth, Delores knew that Agnes had moved on, her sister held to account at last. It sounded like the clock could finally move forward too.

Delores stood alone in front of the fire, rolling Delilah's unfamiliar word around her mouth. *Disruptor.* The word reminded her of Gabriel's tower card and his comment about her planning to topple the hierarchy, bring down governments. It hadn't made sense at the time. She thought the card symbolised Hartigan falling from the chapel, but maybe Gabriel was right about cards having multiple meanings.

'Disruptor,' Delores whispered.

She considered the word for a moment, how it made her feel, then banked it alongside her other favourites: Ernaline, occipital and lepidoptera.

32

While Oddvar slept, Delores, Prudence and Gabriel worked on putting the bookstore back in order, ready to open to the public again. The boxes from the suppliers were unpacked, the tables uncovered and, while Prudence decided what went where, Delores and Gabriel cleaned and stacked and sorted. They didn't mind doing the heavy work or being bossed around, and Prudence pretended not to mind when Delores dropped a book or bumped into tables. Her mother's necromancy was still settling in and every now and then, it knocked her off balance. It was slowly moulding itself into the shape of Delores' own Gift, and she could sense something deep inside her spiralling into it, something she imagined to be like vines, or capillaries or Oddvar's elemental threads. It helped to carry a little of her mother with her, especially at night when her grief felt at its most dangerous.

Prudence had a fresh batch of elixir and Obsidian was teaching her a form of meditation that focused on drawing the feather tips back in when she wished. It was hard work, and she couldn't manage it all the time, but it was giving her some control over her situation. Prudence liked control.

Bartleby was puzzling over some new stripy knitting that Gabriel had cast on for him. His wrists were covered in the same ointment and gauze that Doctor Reid had used to treat Elijah and his favourite blanket had been freshly laundered, but he was still in a bad mood. Everyone at the Tolbooth had accepted that Bartleby would be tricky to handle for some time, but Delores asked him anyway. 'Is there something we can get for you, Barts?'

Bartleby put his knitting down and scratched his chin, as if he hadn't considered this before. 'Oui,' he said, slowly, 'perhaps some blue sherbet straws for le pauvre Monsieur Bartleby?' He sighed, resting his chin on one hand.

Prudence rolled her eyes. 'You still got that cash, Mackenzie?'

Delores checked her trouser pocket for the eternal five-pound note. When she held it in the air, Prudence snapped it up.

'Well Gabriel Galbraith,' said Prudence, 'this is it.

You're coming with us. Sweet Shop Esme misses you. She's ordered some of those salty liquorice sweets you're so keen on, and she's … OK, for a Normal.'

Gabriel opened the door and looked into the street. 'I don't know,' he said, 'maybe next time.'

'Fine,' said Prudence, 'then we all stay inside. With you. Forever.'

Gabriel made a frustrated growling noise, then looked outside again. 'I suppose it is just across the street.'

Prudence grabbed Gabriel's arm before he had chance to change his mind. 'Coming Mackenzie?'

'I'll catch you up,' said Delores. 'There's something I need to do first.'

Obsidian Strange had had his own chair brought from his rooms at the palace and made space for himself next to the fire. His shadow was sitting in Oddvar's chair, swinging its legs. Delores wasn't sure she'd ever get used to that. Shadowmancy was one of Obsidian's Gifts. Delores didn't care to know what his others were.

'I need to speak to you, Uncle,' she said.

Obsidian was so still it was eerie. 'Then speak,' he said at last.

Delores couldn't believe that she was about to

share something so deeply personal with Obsidian Strange. It should be Doctor Reid, or Oddvar, but Delilah had said to trust him. If only she could trust Delilah. 'I have these marks on my skin,' she said, 'but they're not like yours or Doctor Reid's.'

'Go on.'

'When Delilah saw them, she said they were like my dad's and that I should say one word to you.'

'You have my attention.'

Delores took a deep breath. 'Disruptor.'

Obsidian didn't react but his shadow fell out of its chair. It crept along the hearth and crouched next to Obsidian.

Delores shuddered as she took the shadow's recently vacated seat. She was relieved that it still smelled of Oddvar, the scent of fresh hay and old books. It reminded her how it felt to trust.

Obsidian stared at her, pondering. 'What do you understand by that word, Delores?'

Delores shrugged. 'Only what it sounds like. It sounds like trouble.'

Obsidian smiled. 'And trouble is what we are about, Ms Mackenzie. Tell me, just how much trouble can you handle?'

Acknowledgements

Writing this book wouldn't have been half so much fun without the following people, so a huge thanks to…

Penny Thomas and the whole team at Firefly for keeping me the *right side of terrifying.*

Nathan Collins for pushing the spooky boundaries with an unbelievably fiendish cover, and Becka Moor for supernatural design skills.

Onie Tibbit and the Huddlers, Linda Macmillan and the Misfits, Caroline Deacon and the Moniack Mhor Retreaters, the bone-chilling Ghost Gang and the even more chilling WriteMagic Drill Sergeants. Pizza Pals Anneliese Avery and Anna Brooke, writing buddies Michael Mann, Adam Connor, Chrissie Sains, Clare Harlow, Bruna de Luca and Sarah Fulton.

Robbie Donaldson for your help with Gabriel; Charlie, maybe Gabriel will be as bold as you one day, I hope he's already as kind.

Cathy Johnson, Lesley Scriven and Sarah Broadley for the cheer leading and the straight talking. I owe you more cake than Tilly Whitlock could ever bake.

My most fabulous family for still cheering me and my imaginary world onwards, even when bigger and sometimes much scarier life things have been happening.

Hope and Alexandra; Delores and Prudence's origin story. I've stolen a tonne more stuff and I'm not sorry. Love the bones of you.

Kristina, I am sorry about the moths.

And finally, thanks to Terry … for everything.

Yvonne Banham grew up on an island off the coast of Cumbria and spent lots of time huddled on the wild beach with a scary book. When she left school, she couldn't decide whether to be a nurse, an artist, or a writer, so she tried them all and decided she liked words best. She believes in ghosts though she's never met one, and after five gloriously spooky years in Edinburgh, she now lives in Stirlingshire with her husband and their ancient beagle, Toby. When she's not writing, she'll be hiking or trail running in the nearby hills.

You can find out more at
www.yvonnebanhamwrites.com
or follow her @Eviewriter on X.

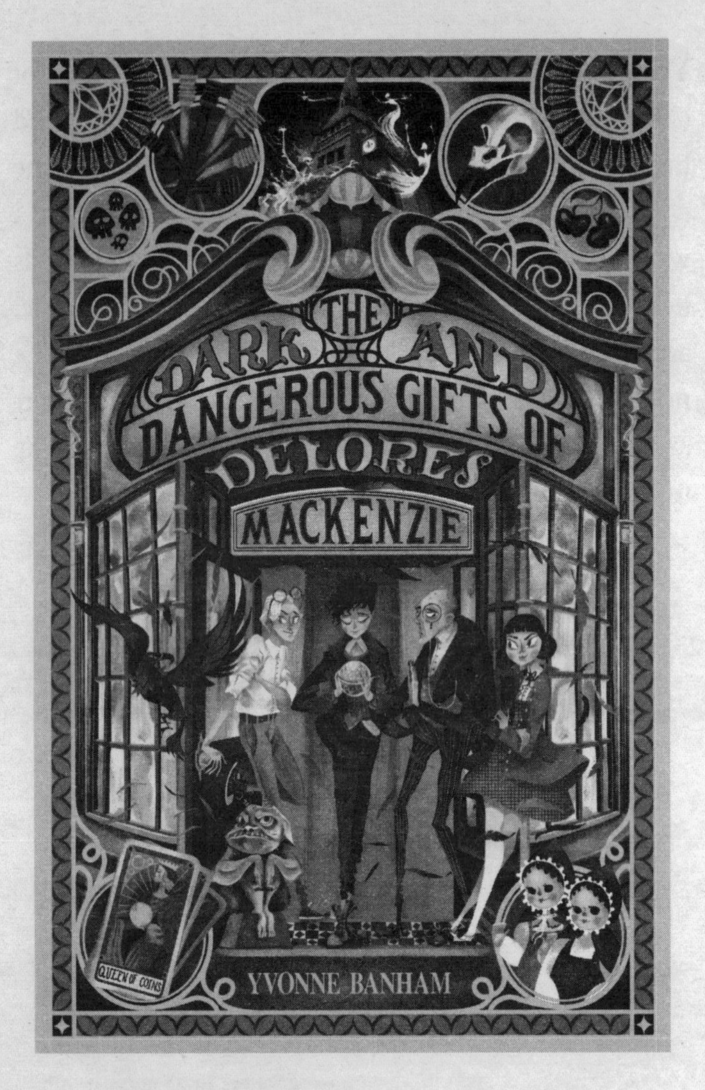

The Dark and Dangerous Gifts of Delores Mackenzie

Yvonne Banham (Firefly, 2023)

ISBN: 978-1-915444-07-3